For Keeps With You

BAXTER BOYS
BOOK FIVE

JESSIE GUSSMAN

Contents

Acknowledgments   v

Chapter 1   1
Chapter 2   6
Chapter 3   13
Chapter 4   19
Chapter 5   26
Chapter 6   30
Chapter 7   40
Chapter 8   50
Chapter 9   60
Chapter 10   69
Chapter 11   75
Chapter 12   82
Chapter 13   90
Chapter 14   100
Chapter 15   107
Chapter 16   111
Chapter 17   120
Chapter 18   128
Chapter 19   134
Chapter 20   142
Epilogue   144

Sneak Peek of The Cowboy's Best Friend   147
A Gift from Jessie   163
*Escape to more faith-filled romance series by Jessie
Gussman!*   165

Acknowledgments

Cover art by Julia Gussman
Editing by Heather Hayden
Narration by Jay Dyess
Author Services by CE Author Assistant

~

Listen to the unabridged audio for FREE performed by Jay Dyess on the Say with Jay channel on YouTube. Get early access to all of Jay's recordings and listen to Jessie's books before they're available to the general public, plus get daily Bible readings by Jay and bonus scenes by becoming a Say with Jay channel member.

Chapter One

Dusty Gibson focused her eyes on the black number two before slamming the visor of her helmet down. The noise of the other competitors faded out, making her feel like she had entered an alternate reality.

Her bike rumbled beneath her.

The two changed to a one.

She flicked her wrist, twisting the handle and pumping the gas. With her other hand, she squeezed the clutch. Her bike trembled in eager anticipation.

The one turned sideways.

Two seconds later, the gates fell. Dusty dropped the clutch and twisted her wrist. Engines screamed around her. Grabbing the clutch, she jerked her foot, caught second, and sprang ahead. A guy in purple on her left edged closer. On her right, a yellow jersey and a red jersey fought for position.

She jammed third, then fourth gear, keeping her eyes on the first jump. Ideal position would be the leader of the pack at that point. She hadn't gotten to be the points leader in motocross racing by running in the back.

Running wide open, she angled to the left, toward purple shirt who was running even with her. From her practice runs, she knew the direct middle of the jump had a slight dip that, hit the wrong way, could cause her bike to flip end over end. Not what she wanted to have happen with a whole class of fifteen aggressive racers behind her.

Purple shirt gave the space then pushed back. Dusty jerked to avoid smacking his foot peg.

Her bike caught; her handlebars twisted. She jerked them back, keeping the throttle on wide open. Sweat trickled down her forehead. The visor on her helmet steamed up, fogging her vision. She could see the horizon where blue met brown but couldn't judge the distance to the first jump. Fifty feet? Thirty?

She needed to get out of the middle. Pushing again at purple shirt, she refused to allow anything but cool determination to sit in her chest. She'd done this a thousand times before. But purple shirt either didn't see her or was determined to keep her boxed in.

The latter was quite possible, since she was the current points leader and, hence, the person to beat.

Her bike screamed beneath her. She twisted hard on the throttle, keeping it wide open. She wanted to catch a big lift on that jump. But not from the middle.

Changing up, she pushed against yellow shirt on her right. But red shirt ran tire to tire with him, and he couldn't give her the space if he wanted to.

She tried purple shirt again. Still no budging.

In a split second, her three options ran through her brain: force purple shirt to move, with contact, if necessary, risking a crash for both of them; slow down, let him and red and yellow go by, which was surely the plan of the other three leaders; or shift her weight off her front tire and hit the jump flat in the middle. The third option would have been the only one she would have considered, except she couldn't see.

She hadn't expected it to be this hot, and she hadn't put her anti-fog on her visor. Rookie mistake.

A decision had to be made. Fast.

Pushing once more at purple shirt, who didn't budge from her side, she crouched on her pegs and squinted, wanting to get the timing just right. Pulling up would slow her down. Not much, but enough to let the others get ahead. Where she wanted to be. Where she was going to be. Nothing was going to stop her from becoming the first female motocross champion.

Suddenly the jump loomed up in front of her, faster than she had estimated. She stood and leaned back, but she was a millisecond too late.

Her front tire dipped. Her body hitched forward. Her bike kicked up, and she was flung over the handlebars, spread-eagle in the air. Purple shirt had decided at the last minute to move over, giving way to a guy in a blue shirt. She caught it out of the corner of her eye in the split second she hung upside down and backward in the air.

The split second before he crashed into her.

A crack sounded loud in her ears. Pain flared up her back and out both arms. Her body flung wildly.

She saw the next bike coming and tried to twist, but the pain radiated out in sharp spikes, and her mind went black.

~

Four weeks later.

"THIS ONE'S YOURS." Sherri, the office nurse, handed Roland Bryant a folder with a smirk. The harsh florescent lighting in their physical therapy office glanced off the pristine white walls with tasteful overblown photos of palm trees hung in an even spread.

He took the folder as he stood behind the high counter and opened it.

Sherri put one hand on the counter. Her bright red nails sparkled. "They requested 'the best.'" She laughed. "You know what that means." With a lifting of her brows, she walked away.

Roland swallowed his snort. When a client requested "the best," it was almost always because they were "the worst." Not the worst as in the physical worst, but the worst as in the most difficult to deal with. He always got those.

His eyes skimmed over the folder. The client would be waiting in the big room where all the therapy sessions were held, but he always liked a little privacy to familiarize himself with a new patient's background before he met them. Some injuries were so horrific he couldn't contain his grimace. Some were unusual, requiring him to do a quick search or even shoot off a few emails to colleagues, for their advice and opinion on best practices.

Dusty Gibson. Twenty-six. He'd fractured his femur and vertebrae T-11 and T-12 in a motocross race. Roland shuddered. There was a starred note that he was a top contender and insisted that he would race again.

Maybe Roland was "the best," but he wasn't a miracle worker, and Dusty was flipping lucky he wasn't paralyzed.

Yeah. He closed the folder, already picturing in his head exercises that would strengthen the rarely used muscles in the back that would help Dusty until his leg was fully healed.

Normally, Roland worked the best with the patients who were discouraged, who needed someone with a story of their own to breathe hope back into a client who wondered what their life was going to consist of now that they were no longer perfectly whole. That, Roland could do. He just told his own story. Leaving his dead fiancée out of it.

With a last glance to make sure all the proper forms had been signed, he carried the folder out. He glanced inconspicuously around the room. Dusty wouldn't be the older gentleman nor the three senior ladies scattered through the room. A skinny elementary school-aged boy sat beside a woman, his mother presumably, with his arm in a brace and his ball cap pulled down over his forehead.

Roland's eyes skimmed over all of those. Dusty would have a leg brace; he might even be in a wheelchair. Only two people in the patient waiting corner of the large room could possibly be twenty-eight years old. A man who did not have a leg cast and a slim woman with waist-length blond hair who did.

She also wore a back brace.

Dusty Gibson, motocross champion, was a woman.

Roland dealt with men, women, boys, girls, old men, and senior ladies. So the odd reaction of his heart, which twisted in his chest, was unexpected. And unwelcome.

He put his game face on. "Dusty Gibson."

The blond rose stiffly, which is the only way one could move in a back brace. She turned. Roland's heart twisted again. Harder. Her wide blue eyes turned in his direction, looking for the source of the summons. A heart-shaped face, cute nose, and high cheekbones complimented that long, straight hair. Her carriage was proud, and despite the braces, she moved with a catlike grace.

No wheelchair. She wasn't even using crutches. He obviously hadn't studied her chart in enough depth.

He pointed to the first counseling room along the side. "We're going there. Let me grab your chart." It wasn't the way he normally met patients, but Dusty had already turned his "normal" upside down, and he hadn't even introduced himself yet.

In the course of his practice as a physical therapist, he'd had a few patients that had stuck with him, because of the severity of their injuries, their amazing personalities, or their grit and determination. He knew for sure Dusty was going to be one of those patients he didn't forget.

Grabbing her chart, he caught up to her in time to open the counseling room door for her.

She gave him a disdainful look. "I can get it myself."

"I'm sure you can."

"Don't patronize me."

She wasn't the first person who came in for therapy with a bad attitude. Now wasn't the time for tough love. That would come soon enough. "I'm sorry," he said.

She walked through the door without another word. He followed, closing it behind him.

Chapter Two

Dusty wanted to fling herself down in the light blue plastic seat, but her back and leg both still hurt, and she wasn't going to fling herself anywhere for a while. So she sat. Gingerly. Hating the fact that her once agile and strong body was crippled and painful.

It wasn't the therapist's fault, though. "I'm sorry I snapped at you," she said grudgingly as the man dressed in khaki pants and a blue polo with the logo of the therapy place in white letters on his shirt stopped in front of her.

"It's okay. I know this isn't where you want to be."

She snorted. "Not even close."

"So that's my job. To get you better so you don't have to come here anymore."

The guy was affable and not bad-looking. She gave him a half smile. "Let's get started."

"I think that's my line."

"You gotta be fast if you want to beat me."

"Let's start at the beginning, then." He held out his hand. "I'm Roland, and I'm going to be coordinating your therapy for the next six months or so."

She smirked, grabbing his proffered hand. "I'm Dusty, and I'm going to do one month, maybe six weeks of this crap, then I'm going back on the circuit." She met his eyes while she spoke. Deep and solid green, they seemed to be searching straight into her soul. Something about his expression, his firm, warm handshake, his confident bearing —she wasn't sure what it was, but she trusted him immediately, which was unusual for her. Usually people had to prove themselves to her.

He blinked, pulling his hand away. Instead of walking around and sitting on the other side of the desk that took up most of the small room, he perched on the corner of it, on her side.

"Are you comfortable in that chair?" he asked.

"Not really."

He jerked his head at the chair behind the desk. "Sit there. It'll be a lot easier on your back and leg."

She didn't appreciate the command given without even a modification in the way of a "please." But in her current state, it was hard to get comfortable, and she'd take what she could get.

"Thank you," she said, standing carefully. He made no move to help her. Not that she could blame him after she about snapped his head off when he opened the door for her. She gimped around and sat in the big, comfortable office chair.

"There's a stool there to prop your leg on."

She looked down, and sure enough, a small wooden stool poked out from under the desk. "Thanks."

His head was bent over her chart. "You're welcome," he said without lifting his head.

She could tell him what was in the chart. That she'd fractured two vertebrae and her femur. Torn ligaments in her knee and right shoulder. Bruised five ribs. Was lucky to be walking.

Whatever. The season was going on without her, and she wanted to get back out. She had been so close to being the first woman to ever win the big championship. She hated feeling that slip through her fingers. Technically, so far, she'd only missed three points races. Even though she hadn't raced, she was still fifth in the standings. She could still pull off a win. And how much sweeter it would be winning after coming back from such a massive setback.

The seconds ticked away. Dusty resisted the urge to squirm. She wasn't used to sitting still this long.

When he finally looked up, he didn't ask any of the questions she'd been expecting. "Where's your ride?"

She rolled her eyes. It was written right in her chart that she wasn't allowed to drive. "My friend dropped me off. She had some errands to run and a baby and toddler that will fare much better at the park down the road than in the waiting room here."

"I'd like to meet her when she picks you up."

She glared at him. "That's your way of making sure I didn't ride my Harley here?"

His eyebrows lifted a fraction. *Ha.*

"I hadn't considered that you might ride your Harley to your first outpatient physical therapy session after breaking your back, your femur, bruising your ribs, and ripping ligaments in your knee and shoulder." He tilted his head. "My bad."

She snorted, trying to keep her lips from quirking up. "It's easy to underestimate me."

"I'll keep that in mind." He tapped the chart. "I see you just got permission today to walk on that leg. It's only been four weeks. Did you have the doctor in a headlock when he wrote that?"

She pursed her lips. "No." She waited a beat. "I had him pinned to the floor with his arm twisted back and up around his ear." Crossing her arms over her chest, she waited.

He nodded like she'd told him the truth. "Another thing to keep in mind."

Her eyes ran over his torso and noted how his biceps strained against the sleeves of his polo shirt. She wasn't going to manhandle him. Not that she was used to winning in physical contests. Soaking wet, she might weight one hundred ten pounds. No, if she wanted to beat the boys, she had to do it on her bike.

And right now, she needed this guy to help her. "Listen, the doc at my appointment today didn't really want me walking without the crutches. But my femur wasn't a compound fracture, it was just a crack, and the x-rays clearly show that a good solid bit of bone has formed over the split. The best thing I can do for it is to start using it regularly."

His lips thinned, but he didn't argue with her. She appreciated that quality in a man.

"Well, you definitely surprised me when you're only four weeks out and don't have crutches." He crossed his arms over his chest. His shirt stretched tight. Dusty kept her eyes pointed up at his face. "A wheelchair wouldn't have surprised me." He wiggled the folder that was under his arm. "I definitely knew I needed to go back and read your chart in detail." His jaw stuck out. "Some clients I have to motivate to move, and some I have to hold back. I know what category you belong to."

"Me too. And you're not holding me back. There's a big race in six weeks, and I'm planning on being in it."

His mouth tightened, and his eyes slid away, but, again, he didn't argue. Good.

"You've got to understand, Dusty, that doing too much can be just as detrimental as not doing enough. I'm on board to get you up and moving like you're used to, without pain, as fast as we can. I'll work with you as hard as I can. But in return, you've got to promise me that you're not going to jeopardize our progress by pushing farther than I say you can."

He raised his brow. She dropped her eyes. Everything in her was on "go fast." She didn't really have another speed. But again, that feeling that she could trust him sat like a comforting hand on her shoulder.

"Dusty, you broke your back. You're very lucky we're talking about getting back normal motion instead of me teaching you how to empty your catheter bag."

She jerked her head. "It didn't happen, and we're not talking about it."

"I think you can regain full motor function, and I think you can live pain-free for the most part. But only if you do this right. You've got great reports from your surgeries and from the hospital therapists. Let's do this thing right, Dusty."

She found herself nodding before she even realized it. "Okay. I'll do what you say."

"That's the attitude." He stood. "Let's go out and get started."

She struggled to her feet.

"I'm going to show you some exercises you can do at home. You're going to be in here every day for a few weeks, but you can still practice at home, in the afternoon if your appointment is in the morning or in the morning if you're seeing me in the afternoon."

"Always you?"

He opened the door and held it for her.

"I get the tough cases."

She smirked then looked pointedly at his hand on the door. "Thank you."

He smiled, showing a strong jaw and straight, white teeth. "You're welcome."

HE'D DEFINITELY BEEN RIGHT that Dusty was going to challenge him. Constantly pushing to do more, even when he could see the lines of pain tightening her eyes and mouth.

It was funny. Some patients he had to practically whip to get them to do what needed to be done. With Dusty, he needed a bridle and a set of reins to pull back on with all his might, and even then, he wasn't sure he could slow her down.

"You can do this one on a step," he said, leading her to the small, sturdy stair they used that was free. Other therapists with other clients were working all around, but he was used to it, and it didn't bother him. Dusty was single-mindedly focused on doing every exercise correctly and for as long as she could. He wasn't even sure half the time she remembered he was around.

She had her game face on now as she watched him demonstrate. "This will help strengthen the ligaments that the surgeon repaired in your knee." He'd already learned that if he told her ten reps, she did fifteen. So he instructed her to do two-thirds as many as he wanted, hiding his satisfied smile when she did exactly what he expected and did almost the exact number he wanted her to do to begin with.

Their entire session went like that. Somehow the hour flew by.

He was showing her the last exercise when Dusty got a big smile on her face and waved. He blinked. Dusty wearing a full-on smile was gorgeous.

Shoving that unprofessional thought clear out of his head, he looked over at the door. A woman with two toddlers—one with tight, curly hair as black as night and one with hair as red as her mother's. The woman waved back.

"Do you need to tell her you'll be a minute?"

"No." Dusty imitated the position he'd shown her and did the exercise perfectly.

A couple of minutes later, she straightened.

"Give me a minute, and I'll get you a sheet printed with all the exercises you'll need to do this evening or tonight." He paused and waited until Dusty met his eyes. "Don't overdo it."

She smiled sweetly. "I won't."

He wasn't fooled by that sweet smile. He narrowed his eyes. "Did you take your prescription pain pills?"

Her smile disappeared. "No. And I won't. I'll deal with the pain. I can't risk getting addicted."

He shook his head. "At least take some over-the-counter stuff. You can take two different kinds as long as they don't have the same active ingredient." He tilted his head and gave his most charming smile. "This will be a lot easier on you if you take the edge off at least."

Her lips pulled back, but her smile did not reach her eyes. "I'll consider it."

It was probably the best he was going to get from her. "I'll be back in a minute with your printout."

"Okay." She turned and gimped to her friend.

He went over to his laptop and typed up the session notes. Then he grabbed the exercises she needed and printed them out. Putting them in a folder, he walked over to Dusty and the red-haired woman.

"Roland, this is Harris Baxter. Harris, this is my torturer, Roland. Apparently, he's the best they have here."

Roland's brow went up with that introduction, but he shook Harris's hand. "Nice to meet you, ma'am."

"It's good to meet you too." Harris was soft-spoken, and Roland wondered how someone like Dusty could have a friend like Harris. They seemed to be opposites. "I'm supposed to ask you how long until Dusty can ride her Harley to therapy."

"Dusty and I have already had a whole conversation about her Harley."

"And you neglected to mention when I could start riding it." Dusty crossed her arms over her chest.

He held her eyes. No one had apparently told her what it said in big, bold letters at the bottom of her file, although someone should have. Maybe she was in denial? Or maybe she didn't realize he knew. "Not this week. Let's leave it at that and go from there next week, okay?"

Her lips flattened, but she said, "Okay."

With a little girl's hand in each one of her own, she hobbled slowly out the door. He watched her go, her long, blond ponytail swinging below her waist. Obviously, there was something in her past driving her. He felt a kindred spirit in that regard. But one of the first lessons he'd learned was to not get too attached to his patients. His job was to fix them and let them go.

Dusty would be devastated when she learned what her chart said, if she didn't already know, but he wasn't going to tell her. Her doctor should have already done that, but if he didn't, Roland wasn't going to push in. Not only might it demoralize her, but it was possible she could give up altogether. Let her strive for the goal. And let her doctor deliver the bad news.

Chapter Three

Dusty sat on the park bench with her friend, Cassidy Baxter and watched the sun come up. The western sky glowed a pretty pink and blue, while the eastern sky exploded in glorious orange color that reflected off a long, thin layer of clouds. The shallow reservoir in front of her glowed in muted reflection, and orange shone off the shiny plastic monkey bars and the silver slide.

Before her accident, when her schedule allowed, she and Cassidy had made a point to meet in the early morning and walk together. Their town wasn't huge, and the park wasn't terribly busy, but it was a popular place for joggers and walkers in the morning.

"I'm sorry you're missing your exercise time."

Cassidy shrugged like it didn't matter. "Don't worry about it."

Dusty didn't have children, but her best friends were all married with small kids, and she knew that even a few minutes to take a short walk was precious with the little ones around.

Cassidy put a hand on Dusty's shoulder. "I have the rest of my life to walk. When I first heard about your accident, I thought I would be spending the rest of my life walking alone." She tilted her head, doing the parent thing with her eyebrows, trying to make Dusty feel guilty for making her worry. It worked.

"Torque enjoys spending mornings with the kids, and he likes knowing that I'm spending time with a friend. So don't apologize."

"Give me a couple of weeks, and we'll be back walking." The park road which they walked on made a big half-mile loop around the trees and creek and playground and scattered pavilions and reservoir.

"With the help of your handsome therapist?" Cassidy bumped her shoulder but kept her eyes on the sunrise.

"Yep." Dusty didn't take the bait. "With his help, and the help of my doctors and surgeons and my friends." She didn't mention her parents. They were in their big motor home, heading back from Arizona. Her mother had flown in right after her accident, but she'd left after a week or two.

Dusty was their late-in-life "oops." With two brothers who were almost twenty years older than she was, she grew up pretty much alone, always knowing that she was the only thing keeping her parents from enjoying their empty nest.

"Harris said the guy was pretty good-looking."

"Does Turbo know she's looking at other men?" Dusty asked lightly. Turbo adored his wife. The adoration was mutual and sometimes annoying for their friend who wasn't married.

"Harris is a natural-born matchmaker."

"She found a new skill?" Dusty couldn't remember anyone Harris had actually helped get together. Now, Turbo's brother Tough on the other hand...maybe he wasn't exactly a matchmaker, but since he wrote a syndicated romance advice column, he was definitely knowledgeable about relationships. Even if he didn't talk much.

Cassidy shrugged. "You're changing the subject. Is your therapist good-looking?"

"In a not-for-me-because-he's-too-soft kind of way." A little line of guilt shot down her sore back, but Dusty ignored it. Roland was gorgeous, and he definitely wasn't soft.

"Hmm? What does that mean? Harris said he looked like he could throw you over his shoulder and haul you away if he wanted to."

"Yeah, any seventh grader could do that." Dusty rolled her eyes. She'd been skinny and straight as a beanpole her whole life. Not that it bothered her. When she had her helmet on, everyone thought she was a young boy. Which was fine. She didn't want any special treatment just because she was female. Especially on the track.

Cassidy chuckled. "Okay. Fine. Don't tell your best friend about your cute, unmarried therapist."

"I never asked him if he was married." Dusty's eyes widened, and she kept her head turned to the sunrise that was fading from the sky so Cassidy wouldn't know.

"Harris said he wasn't wearing a ring."

"You know, I don't care what the doctors say, I'm driving myself to my next therapy session. Harris spent more time checking the guy out than I did."

"So you did check him out?"

Busted. Cassidy made a great lawyer.

"He's cute." She shrugged. "Okay? I admit it. The guy is cute, and he's nice, and he seems knowledgeable about what he's doing. I specifically demanded that my doctor request the best, and he's what they gave me. But, come on. He's a professional. And right now, I'm hardly attractive with these bulky braces."

Cassidy flipped Dusty's ponytail. "This blond hair is striking wherever you are."

It was her only feminine attribute. She didn't have hips, and she didn't have boobs. She didn't have time for makeup, even if she knew how to put it on, and she hated shopping, so her wardrobe was simple and functional. But she did make time for her hair.

"I don't want a guy who falls in love with long, blond hair. There's a lot more to me than my hair."

"But your hair would catch his eye. Make him look twice, and maybe he'd notice all the realness beneath the hair."

"I want to win the championship. I'm not really interested in cute guys."

Cassidy didn't say anything, and Dusty appreciated it. Most guys couldn't take her competitive streak. And that was fine with her. Maybe it had to do with her parents never seeming to want her, but none of the superficial boyfriends she'd had ever seemed to really want her for herself. Maybe she was a self-fulfilling prophecy—she and Harris and Cassidy and their other friend, Kelly, had more than one discussion about Dusty's inability to trust a guy when he said he'd stay.

"Well, Harris seemed impressed with this one. I want to meet him."

"He wears polo shirts, and his hands don't have callouses on them. I could ride circles around him on my bike. He's not for me." She was such a liar. Of course, it was true that she had never been attracted to the Yale-type white-collar professional man look. But Roland rocked it. And his compassionate personality, essential for his job, pulled at her. "There's some kind of rule somewhere that says you can't have a relationship with your therapist anyway."

"I think that's your shrink."

Dusty laughed. "Quit it. You know it's true. Just like you couldn't have a relationship with your client. Probably not with a judge, either."

"You're probably right, but I don't have to worry about that since Torque has no plans to give up his garage and put on a black robe." Cassidy tilted her head. "Although he'd look good in one."

Dusty snorted, her eye caught by a figure jogging on the other side of the reservoir. It wasn't really that he looked familiar, but it was more that he wore jogging pants rather than shorts like the other joggers. They'd seen him before from a distance as they walked, but it had been cooler. Now that it was June and the weather had warmed, it seemed odd that he was still dressed like it was early spring.

"One of my associates at the courthouse wants to learn to fly." Cassidy's words made Dusty jerk her eyes away from the jogger. Something about him nagged at her.

Cassidy continued. "You took lessons for a while, didn't you?"

"I have. Motocross has taken most of my time, but I'd love to get back to it." She loved flying, but her competitive nature had gotten sucked into the efforts to win a championship. She'd have to make time to get back in the air.

"Was your instructor good? I told my associate I'd ask you for a recommendation. He thinks he'll have to go to Pittsburgh for a good flight instructor."

"No! I took lessons from Whiff at the regional airport outside of town, and he was really great. I loved him. Very calm and knowledgeable." Dusty took her eyes off the jogger to dig her phone out of her pocket. "I'm sure I still have his contact."

She punched it up and shot off a text with the info to Cassidy.

"There. You should have it now. I highly recommend him."

"Thanks."

Dusty's eyes went back to the jogger. What was it about him?

Then his head turned, glancing at the sunrise, and the angle of his jaw tripped the memory in her brain. "That's him."

"Huh?" Cassidy said, her gaze on the sky where only a bit of orange still glowed against the blue.

"I think that's my therapist."

Cassidy's eyes snapped to Dusty before going to the man across the water. "The jogger?" Cassidy asked, even though he was the only man in sight.

"Yep."

"That guy jogs here almost every day. We've seen him a lot before. You didn't recognize him?" Cassidy asked.

"No. I never pay attention."

"That's true. We're usually talking so much, I just throw a hand up to wave and never really look at the people we pass." Cassidy stared thoughtfully. "It's hard to see from here, but he looks built. He's not a slacker if he's up this early."

The jogger turned his head back, but then, for some reason, maybe he felt their eyes on him, he looked out over the water. Dusty jerked, like his gaze had shocked through her. He couldn't recognize her from over there, she thought, just as he raised his hand in a wave. She returned his greeting. Had he recognized her?

"You recognized *him*," Cassidy said, and Dusty realized she'd asked that question out loud. "It was probably the hair; it's usually behind your back, but today it's hanging down in front. Hard to miss."

Dusty fingered her hair as the jogger disappeared into the woods.

"Come on. Let's go get some coffee before we head home." Dusty lifted herself slowly off the bench, appreciating the fact that Cassidy didn't try to help.

"You know, just because the guy doesn't have a death wish like you do doesn't mean he wouldn't make a great husband and father. And you can give me your tough-girl attitude all you want, but that's what you want. A guy who's going to stick with you. Don't dismiss him because he doesn't come from the world you rotate in."

Dusty compressed her lips and didn't answer as she limped down the path toward Cassidy's car. Cassidy very politely didn't point out that Dusty came from wealth and privilege. She wasn't born with a wrench in her hand. It was what she wanted, an easy way to get attention, maybe, and her parents had indulged her.

It really didn't matter. She wasn't giving it up, and she couldn't see a guy like Roland in the stands at one of her races. He'd stand out like a blue pumpkin in a field of orange.

Chapter Four

Roland checked the time. Dusty should be coming in any second. He knew the schedule, and he knew which clients were on it, so just because he knew Dusty should be walking through that door did not mean he was interested in her for any more than the client-patient relationship.

But he had thought about her. He wasn't sure if the woman in the park this morning was her or not. But the blond hair stood out, even across the water in the early morning light. Maybe he just wanted it to be her.

He'd spent the hours since he'd seen her lecturing himself on how he needed to be professional. Keep that distance between them. Do the job he'd been hired to do. The one he was good at.

Sherri waved him over. He checked again for Dusty before walking to her desk. She pressed a button on her office phone, probably Mute, before she spoke, low and excited. "Remember those two mountain bikers you worked with last summer?"

Roland nodded. They were professors at a college in Florida but had come to Pennsylvania and rented a house because they'd wanted to bike in the Appalachians. They hadn't been injured, but they'd gone to him for strength training exercises to avoid injury. Nice guys. They'd loved his work and had taken him out for dinner the last night before they went back to Florida. They still called once in a while.

"I have a ski instructor on the phone who says they recommended you to him. He wants you to go out to Colorado and spend three to four weeks working with his clients." Sherri lowered her voice even further. "*High-end* clients." Like he didn't know it, she added, "This would be great for our practice. Craig wants to expand."

But Roland was already shaking his head. "If they come in here, I'll work with them as much as they want. I'm not flying out." He wasn't flying. Full stop.

"I know your position," Sherri said. "And I already told him. They can't fly in." She gave him a prodding look. "This would be fabulous for your career."

"No." He said it firmly and clearly. He was not flying. Not ever again. He'd barely survived the last time. Janice didn't.

Sherri's face fell, but she nodded. His attitude about flying was not a secret. He didn't care how much it hurt his career.

He walked away, looking around for Dusty, putting the opportunity he was missing out of his head. It wasn't worth it.

Dusty walked in. Alone again. He smiled a little to himself, wondering if her Harley was parked in the lot but fairly certain it wasn't. She was a risk-taker and a little untamed, which was hugely attractive to him, kind of like his former fiancée, but she wasn't stupid.

Pain squeezed his heart. He hadn't thought of Janice in a while, but he'd never recover from losing her. Some things just couldn't be erased out of a human brain. The screams of his loved one as she lay trapped and burning to death were one of those things.

Maybe he was attracted to Dusty's untamed nature, but it repulsed him at the same time. He could never put himself in a relationship again where he was constantly worried about his partner. He'd been to enough funerals. He'd also seen enough in his job about what happened to the risk-takers. They ended up in the waiting room, wanting him to get them moving again, so they could go right back out and do whatever dangerous thing had landed them there to begin with. No thanks.

"Dusty Gibson," he called. She stopped walking toward the waiting area chairs and turned, her eyes finding him.

He gave his best professional smile. "Come on. Let's get started."

Normally he worked with several clients at once. But often with the first few sessions of therapy, he started clients one-on-one, especially the more challenging cases. Dusty definitely belonged in that category.

She limped over. The big brace on her leg was uncomfortable and bulky. It was enough to frustrate most people. But then she had the back brace on as well. She had to feel claustrophobic in all that.

"How'd your exercises go?"

"Fine."

"Sore?"

"A little."

She seemed a little depressed. He was supposed to note in the file if the client's mental health seemed off. He'd give her a few minutes. There had been a few patients over the years who had just never warmed up to him for whatever reason. Maybe Dusty would be one of them.

"You didn't ride your Harley in, did you?"

A little smile ghosted her lips. "Nope."

"That's good. I'd hate to have to note that in your chart."

"I didn't drive either." She pushed her ponytail over her shoulder.

"That's good to know." Although a car would be preferable to the bike. Either one would be a real challenge with that brace. "Let's get started."

He put her through the exercises he'd given her and taught her a few that he'd looked up online. She did them with the same concentration and determination that she'd shown the previous day.

Toward the end of the session, she still wasn't smiling.

"You seem down. Are you in pain?" He didn't want to have to make a note and have her hauled off to a therapist if she didn't need it.

"No, I'm fine."

He crossed his arms and looked at her. "You would tell me if this is too much for you?"

"Probably not," she answered. He liked that honesty.

When she didn't say anymore, he considered taking her into the consulting room and telling her his story. It was part of his job. Usually it helped clients to know that he understood exactly what they were going through. It was an encouragement, especially to the ones that weren't motivated or were depressed. Dusty didn't have a problem with lack of motivation.

For some reason, he didn't want to show his vulnerability to Dusty. Deciding she wasn't depressed and didn't need his life story, he finished their session without prying further. He'd wait and see how she was the next day.

A different friend came to pick her up. Bubbly and blond, she had three small children with her. Did all of Dusty's friends have families? And where were her parents? Even middle-aged people usually had their parents around.

He chided himself. It was only her second day. But there was the red-haired friend from yesterday. The brown-haired friend on the park bench, if that was even Dusty. And now, a blond. At least she had variety in her friends' hair color.

"Roland, this is Kelly." Dusty introduced him when he came over with her instruction paper.

Then he realized where he'd seen her before. "You're Tough Baxter's wife." Tough Baxter was his mechanic, which reminded him he needed to schedule an oil change.

She nodded with a big smile. "Sure am." Grabbing his hand, she pumped it. "You've also donated some time to work with kids at the children's centers I run."

He studied her, thinking. "I don't remember seeing you there." The different therapists usually donated a month of after-work time. He always made sure his month was in the winter. Usually January. It was a very unofficial thing, but kids could always benefit from learning exercises that would straighten their posture or help prevent carpal tunnel. He'd show them stretches and explain the benefits of staying flexible. Then there were always those few children who could use more specialized care. He did his best and enjoyed working with the children, giving them tools they could use for the rest of their lives.

"No. I typically arrange things, secure funding, sometimes drop in and watch to make sure everything is going okay. I even pick kids up and drop them off. But I don't get involved in things I don't know anything about. Like physical therapy."

He nodded, aware that Dusty was watching him. He turned to her, while Kelly's children tugged at her hands. "Here's your printout. Same drill as yesterday. Do these this afternoon or this evening, and I'll see you again tomorrow."

"Yes, sir." She didn't salute but allowed the kids tugging at her hands to drag her out the door.

⁓

BY THE END of her first two weeks of outpatient therapy, Dusty was ready to quit. It felt like she wasn't getting anywhere.

She walked in after Cassidy dropped her off even more dejected than usual. She was putting her friends out, getting rides every day. Riley, Ben Baxter's wife, was going to use her lunch break to pick her up, which made Dusty feel awful. Even though Riley had only been in the area a little over a year, Dusty loved her like a sister. Still, it was bad enough to put her lifelong friends out. Even worse was taking advantage of her good friends, too. By the time this was over, people weren't going to be answering the phone when she called.

"Dusty Gibson, bring your smile over here."

She rolled her eyes, and yes, her lips turned up at Roland's cheesy call. When she got close enough to him, she said, "Do people ever ignore you because you're so embarrassing?"

"Nope." He stopped. "Well, not that I know of. Sometimes I just assume people aren't here."

She laughed, probably as he intended. More than being concerned with just her physical well-being, he seemed to keep a finger on the pulse of her emotions too. It should bother her, because it was none of his business, but her brain had decided to trust him the first time she was here, and it hadn't changed its mind.

They went through her exercises easily and finished early. "If you don't mind, I'd like to spend a few minutes in the consulting room."

She shrugged. Did it really matter if she minded?

She followed him to the middle room, not even taking the bait when he smirked and opened the door for her. She breezed through.

No. In her mind, she breezed through. In reality, she limped painfully and slowly through the door, moving around the desk to sit in the comfortable chair on the other side.

He didn't even bother to hide his grin.

She propped her leg up. "What? Were you going to make the poor crippled girl sit in the uncomfortable chair?"

He shook his head slowly, his grin fading. "They ought to get better chairs in here."

Like every time before, he leaned on the edge of the desk. "Tell me what the trouble is. I can't fix what I don't know is broken."

Straight to the point. She could respect that.

She leaned forward, clasping her hands and twitching at the pain in her back and leg. "Fine." She shrugged. "It's not helping. It's been six weeks since my accident, three weeks since my surgeries. I'm still in pain, and I'm sick of bumming rides from my friends. Almost as sick as they must be of giving them. I want to see results." She looked up and met his clear, green eyes. "I've been doing every single thing you said. And I've been doing it faithfully. I haven't shirked or skipped. I've fought through the pain, and frankly, it's depressing to not see any improvement."

"We measured your range of motion in your knee. It's improved fifteen percent just in this week."

"I want to lose the brace."

"Only the doctor can do that for you. You have an appointment Monday, right?"

She wasn't Roland's only patient. How did he keep these facts in his head? Maybe because he'd just studied her chart before she came in. He hadn't looked at it since, although it was tucked under his arm as he sat on the corner of the desk with his arms crossed.

"That's right."

"I can make a note on your chart that you've been excelling with your exercises and following your instructions to the letter. I've already written down your improved range of motion. You still have pain, but am I wrong in calculating that it's not as bad?"

She thought back. He was right. "Those back strengthening exercises have helped."

"They're designed to train the muscles that support your spine. It takes some of the pressure off and helps with the pain."

"It has, I guess." She looked down.

"Is that what's really bothering you?"

For some reason, his question brought tears to her eyes. She kept her eyes down on her lap where she picked at her fingers.

She sighed, blinking back the annoying weakness of tears. "There was a race today. I should be checked in and doing my practice laps. Instead, I'm stuck here, barely able to move and dependent on my friends to haul me around."

Roland didn't move, and he didn't say anything. She appreciated the time to get her features composed.

Finally she looked up. "I'm sorry my bad attitude was so awful that you noticed. I was just a little down about the race, but I'm still committed to pounding out these exercises and getting better."

He nodded, his brows drawn together. "I really don't think your friends mind taking you around. They love you and appreciate this opportunity to do something for you. Isn't that how you'd feel if your positions were reversed?"

Guilt made her bow her head again. "It is. I'm the one that resents my loss of freedom."

"I wish I could make this process easier or faster, but in order to do it right, it has to be like this."

She put her hand up. "I know. That's why I've tried not to complain. But you asked."

He grunted a laugh. "That's true. I did."

She lifted her head up. "You just don't understand what it's like."

Chapter Five

Roland stared at Dusty. This was his opening. He could tell her about the long process and encourage her to stick with it. He'd never hesitated before. Why was he hesitating now?

He shoved whatever feeling it was aside and straightened off the desk. "That's where you're wrong." He moved around the side of the desk. "Do you have a weak stomach?"

Her brows drew down into a V. "Huh?"

He reached down for the bottom of his pant leg. "I showed this to one woman, and she threw up on me." He turned his head and looked up at her with one eye. "I'm not making that up."

"Showed her what?" Dusty asked, her brows still drawn.

He pulled his pant leg up. The pink and white deformed skin slowly came into view. He set his foot on the desk. "This." He lifted a shoulder. "This is actually my good leg."

"You're kidding." Dusty gasped, throwing a hand over her mouth. "I'm sorry," she said between her fingers.

"It's fine. You should hear the kids' reactions."

Her eyes snapped to his. "You tell them?"

"If I think they need to hear it."

Her hand dropped back to her lap. "So I need to hear it?"

"You said I didn't understand." He nodded at his leg. Even now, he could hardly believe that it belonged to him. It didn't look like his. "I think I do."

Her fingers twisted in her ponytail, and she bit her lip as her eyes slid slowly back to his leg. She swallowed. "I guess you must."

"Yeah." He dropped his leg down. "You want to see the other one?"

Her eyes flew to his. It was the first time since they'd met that she seemed uncertain. She didn't wear the emotion well.

"Never mind." He put his other leg up and drew up his pant leg. The skin on this leg was even more deformed. It actually turned his stomach.

"Can't they do...surgery, like plastic surgery, to fix that?" she asked. He hated the hesitation in her voice.

"They could. They wanted to, actually. But I'd already spent months, *months*, in the hospital. Skin grafts. Bandage changes. Infections. Constant pain. I was ready to walk out and never walk into another hospital again."

"I bet." Now compassion filled her eyes, and he didn't like that any better. He shoved his pant leg down and dropped his foot.

"How old were you?" she asked.

"I was a second-year medical student." Normally he stopped the questions right here. But she was faster than his normal patients.

"You were going to be a doctor."

"Yeah." He shifted, leaning again on the desk, his arms crossed over his chest. "A hospital's a bad place for a doctor to hate." He shrugged like it didn't matter. "By the time I was done with therapy, I had found a new calling." He met her eyes, keeping any emotional pain wiped clean from his face. "People seem to think I'm good at it."

"I see why." She nodded. Her posture straightened, and her chin lifted. "It worked. Anything boys can do, girls can do better." She grinned with a challenge. "You did it. I can do it better."

He laughed. "I never understood the competition between the sexes, but if that's what motivates you, lap it up."

"You don't compete with your girlfriend?"

His face fell. Technically, he supposed, he'd won because she'd died. But, no, he'd never considered it a competition. Even if she was a med student too. One from a family of means who'd thought it a good idea to let their beautiful, gregarious daughter get her pilot's license. Stupid parents.

"No." He gave her honesty. "I always thought of us as a team with different strengths that complemented each other." He closed his mouth. If he started to think about Janice, the pain he kept locked away might escape.

"Past tense?" she asked softly.

"She died." He stood abruptly. "I bet your friend is waiting on you. Which one is it today? Harris? Or Kelly, Tough's wife?"

Dusty took the hint, thankfully, and struggled out of the chair. "Riley is picking me up. She'll be new."

"You have a lot of friends." He walked to the door and put his hand on the knob.

Dusty nodded. "I guess you could have given me a lecture on counting my blessings."

"Would that have been effective? Because I do have that one in my repertoire."

"Maybe. I guess you can try it out on me next week."

"Okay. I'll keep that in mind. If your doctor's appointment doesn't go well on Monday, I'll brush it off and whip it out."

She laughed. "Oh, it's going to go well. If he knows what's good for him, he's going to tell me I can drive and I can lose at least one of these braces."

"Good luck with that." He bet the doctor actually would allow her to take her brace off and drive. Maybe not with a regular patient, but Dusty was anything but regular.

He opened the door, and she limped out ahead of him. A very pregnant woman with shoulder-length brown hair stood by the door. Her face brightened, and she smiled at Dusty.

"I'll be right over," he said as Dusty limped away.

He wrote his notes and printed off her instruction sheet.

"Roland, this is Riley Baxter."

"Looks like Riley and a plus one." He shook her hand and met her direct gaze.

She laughed. "It feels like I'm carrying a plus thirteen. But the doctor assures me it's only one. Just big, like his dad."

"And ready to show up any day," Dusty said with a grin.

"That's what they said at my appointment today." She sighed with a hand on her large belly. "I'm ready. Anything over sixty-five degrees is too hot when you're pregnant, and it's June. It's time."

"Wait until you get me home first, please." Dusty smiled, but there was a definite shadow of fear in her eyes.

"Dusty, the doctor said you weren't allowed to drive, but there are no restrictions on your chart about delivering babies." Roland couldn't resist teasing her.

"I would be helpless in that situation, I promise," she said with a shudder. "You're not feeling any contractions, are you?"

Riley shook her head. "Unfortunately, no."

"You need to tell him to wait until after tomorrow. It would be awkward to have to cancel your baby shower because he decided to show up."

"Sorry, but if I have to choose between seeing my little guy and having the baby shower, I'm going for my kid."

"I get it. He can come any time after three."

They linked arms, and Dusty turned to wave.

"See you Monday," Roland said, trying not to wonder why he felt this odd sense of sadness at not seeing her for two days.

Chapter Six

Saturday afternoon, Roland pulled his car into the garage. He liked coming to Tough Baxter's garage. Not only because it wasn't too far from where he lived—just a few minutes across town—but also because Tough was an easygoing guy who was just as likely to hand him a wrench and show him how to do something as he was to do it for him.

To someone like him, who had more book knowledge than actual hands-on knowledge, it was a nice change. No one in his family worked a blue-collar job. His dad was a lawyer, his mother an obstetrician, both practicing in Philadelphia. His brother was on the board of some company in Texas. Roland wasn't sure exactly what he did, but he was sure it didn't involve getting his hands any dirtier than a round of golf required.

At Tough's, there were also the old men who were always arguing in the corner. It gave the place character. All around, Tough's garage was a great place to spend a Saturday.

Roland wore old clothes and showed up at twelve on the dot. Although when he'd called, Tough had said "around lunch." Tough was pretty relaxed.

"That's good," Tough said as Roland inched his car forward. "We'll have it on the lift."

"Okay." Roland slid his window up before getting out. When he first started coming, Tough didn't talk as much. Since he'd gotten married, he definitely smiled more. Sentences seemed to come a little easier for him, too. A good woman could have that effect on a man.

He shoved that thought aside before he started thinking about Janice again.

"How ya been, Tough?" Roland held out his hand. Tough grabbed it with his calloused one and pumped.

"Busy."

"It's that time of year. School's letting out, and everyone's getting ready to go on vacation."

One side of Tough's mouth curved up. "Good for business."

"You and me both. Lots of sports injuries in the summer."

"Wow, that's sad." Turbo, Tough's brother, came over, holding a red-haired toddler in one arm and a dark-haired toddler in another. DeShaun, his oldest son, trailed behind. "It must be awful to make your living off the misfortune of others."

Turbo was never serious. In all the time Roland had been at the garage, Turbo was perpetually happy. He took the statement like the joke it was.

"Kind of like a tow-truck driver, huh?"

Turbo laughed. The kids in his arms watched his face and smiled when he did. "We've got a smart aleck on our hands."

"Takes one to know one," one of the old men at the checkerboard shouted across the garage.

"It never fails to amaze me how good their hearing is when I'm not trying to talk to them," Turbo said with a headshake.

"I heard that," the same white-haired guy shouted.

Tough laughed. "You know where the wrenches are. I'll get a filter."

Turbo shifted the kids in his arms. "Seriously? This is the only shop I know where people have to do the work themselves." He looked at Roland. "He'll probably still charge you."

"Double rate when I do the work myself," Roland said with a straight face.

"Triple if he tries to give me advice while he's doing it," Tough said with the same serious look.

Turbo grinned. "Well, I'd love to help, but I'm busy." He jiggled the kids in his arms. "I'm heading over to Kelly's children's center to play for a while." He cleared his throat. "I mean, to let the kids play for a while."

Roland laughed at the idea of Turbo at the children's center that shared the building with Tough's garage. "The truth comes out first, huh?"

"There's nothing wrong with having fun at any age," Turbo said over his shoulder as he walked to Tough's office. The buildings connected through the back office, although Roland had only seen family using the connecting doors.

"At least Kelly can help keep an eye on Turbo. No telling what he'll get into over there," Roland commented as Tough handed him the box with the filter in it.

"Kelly's at a baby shower." Tough snorted. "Along with Turbo's wife and all the other ladies in the family."

"Oh." Roland set the box aside. He'd never really thought much about babies. Even when Janice and he were together, they'd kind of had an understanding that babies would be far in the future after both of them had completed medical school and residencies. His brother was married, and they weren't planning on having children.

Having hit thirty with no kids and no wife, Roland figured he probably would never have any. He really hadn't recovered from losing Janice. He definitely wasn't interested in going through that again.

But a long-haired blond popped into his mind as he twisted the filter wrench. Dusty had impressed him with her drive and determination. She got knocked down but wasn't afraid to get back up and keep trying. Although Dusty was going to have to find something else to do other than motocross racing. Maybe the doctor would break the news to her at her appointment on Monday.

Several hours later, his oil was changed, and he stood around drinking coffee and talking shop with the old men, Tough, and Turbo. The other Baxter brothers, Ben and Torque, had arrived in the early afternoon. Torque had his kids in tow. Roland remembered the shower was for Ben's wife, Riley, who had picked Dusty up from therapy.

"When was her due date again?" Torque asked, taking a sip of his coffee and shaking his head when one of his preschooler twins asked to have a sip.

"Tomorrow," Ben said. He was the only one who didn't have a child in his arms. Every other time Roland had met Ben, he'd seemed pretty calm, but today he couldn't stop pacing.

"I'm betting you're going to get a call to meet her at the hospital," Turbo said with a smirk.

Roland would bet on that too. When she'd picked Dusty up, he'd just hoped she made it out of the therapy center before labor started.

"Shut up, Turbo," Ben said, his calm tone belying his words and the twitching of his leg.

Torque grinned. "There's nothing to it, Ben. You watch your wife suffer in agony for twelve to twenty-four hours, then she can't stop smiling, and you never sleep again. Easy as a medieval torture chamber."

"We could have chosen a torture chamber?" Turbo acted surprised. "I'd have done that. In a heartbeat."

Ben had quit trying to pretend he wasn't pacing. He poured what had to be his seventh cup of coffee.

"You guys aren't making him feel any better," Roland felt compelled to say.

"There's nothing to feel better about," the old man with the white hair, Mr. Sigel, said.

"It hurts, and no amount of Twinkies makes it better," Turbo said with a dramatic shudder.

"You must be talking about labor again." Harris, Turbo's wife, walked in the garage door.

"Busted," Torque said under his breath.

Roland laughed. He saw his brother every other Christmas. They might spend a few minutes talking about the stock market. It wasn't fun, and he couldn't wait to leave. He'd much rather hang out in the garage with the Baxter brothers. But if the wives were home, that was his cue to go.

"I threw my check on your desk," he said to Tough as a blond and a very similar-looking brunette walked in. He wasn't sure, and couldn't remember their names, but he thought those were the Baxter sisters. Twins, if he recalled correctly.

Tough nodded. "Thanks."

Roland threw a hand up as he walked away. "See you guys in a few months."

The brothers called out farewells. He nodded at the twins and Harris and Cassidy and Kelly. He would have nodded a greeting at Riley, but Ben had hurried to her and was hovering over her in a way that Roland, even with his limited experience with pregnant women, could tell was guaranteed to annoy her. He laughed to himself and shut the door behind him, digging in his pocket for the keys to his car which they'd parked along the street to get it out of the way.

A blond head in the back of one of the cars caught his eye. At first, he assumed he was imagining things. For some reason, he seemed to see blond heads everywhere lately. But he slowed down anyway. In the back of his mind, ever since he heard about the shower, he'd wondered if he'd see Dusty.

She had her braced leg propped along the back seat. Her head leaned back against the back window, and her eyes were closed.

Maybe he should have walked by, but he tapped on the window.

She jerked up, wincing.

Immediately, concern tightened his chest.

Her eyes widened when she saw him. She twisted and put her finger up to put the window down.

"Hey," he said. "Riley made it through the shower without anyone having to practice their baby delivering skills?"

Dusty smiled, which was what he was going for. "Yeah. Much to everyone's relief. Mine, most of all."

"Yeah. I can see you taking a bike apart and putting it back together blindfolded, but I have a hard time picturing you delivering a baby."

She smiled, but it was pinched. His health care instincts kicked in.

"You're hurting." He'd found with people like Dusty, it was better to state the obvious, because she'd just deny it if he asked.

She sighed. "My back."

A jolt of concern went through him. Of all of her injuries, her back was the one that could have done the most damage.

"I've been sitting too long, but," she laughed, "it hurts to walk. It hurts to sit. It hurts to stand on my head." She swallowed. "I can't really do anything without pain."

"Someone is coming to take you home?" He wasn't sure whose car she was sitting in.

"I told them to take their time. Hanging out at the garage is downtime combined with family time for them, and I didn't want to rush them."

"I'll take you home." Even as the words were coming out of his mouth, he knew he was blurring the line between therapist and patient. He already thought of Dusty way more than his other clients, and he'd warned himself repeatedly that he needed to be careful.

She looked down, seeming to think about it. He half hoped she'd say no. But there was no denying the excitement that leaped in his soul when she said, "Okay."

"Let me run in and tell them. I'll be back out in a second to give you a hand."

Her head snapped up, and he held up his hand. "I know. I know. You can do it yourself. I'm your therapist, remember?" He felt like he needed the reminder. "But let me help because I want to, and it makes me feel good."

Her lips curved up, and she rolled her eyes. "Fine."

He hurried in. The ladies wanted to come out and talk to her, but he assured them she was fine, and since they all knew him as Dusty's therapist, he got the impression they figured she'd be in good hands.

Dusty was out of the car when he returned. "I thought you said I could help?"

She lifted a slim shoulder. "You weren't here."

"Here." He held out his arm. "Hold onto me and try to keep from putting all your weight on your knee." Her hand came up and squeezed his biceps. He tried to tell himself that didn't give him a thrill, but it was an outright lie. Pointing them in the direction of his car, he started walking, letting her set the pace.

"I assume your ribs don't hurt?" He remembered reading on her chart that they'd been bruised. Sometimes ribs were the slowest thing to heal.

"My whole body feels sore. I overdid it with the shower." She gave him a sideways look. "I tried to help decorate."

He shook his head. "The therapist in me wants to lecture you."

"Ignore him."

"I think that's my feminine side."

"So," she said slowly, "as a therapist, you identify with the female pronouns?"

He laughed outright but stopped abruptly when he glanced over and she wasn't smiling.

"Male pronouns. Every day." His grin teased a smile out of her.

They stopped at the side of his car. "Do you need to sit in the back?" he asked.

"If I take my brace off, I can sit in the front."

"The contents of your chart are confidential, but I think you know the doctor told you to wear it all the time except to shower."

She sighed. A deep sigh that said just how sick of the brace she was.

"You know, if you didn't do dangerous things like race motocross, you wouldn't be wearing a brace right now."

"I'm just as likely to have a car accident and be in worse shape," she replied. Stubbornly in his opinion. It fascinated him how someone so small could have so much determination.

He opened the back door.

"I can fold myself in, but I look like a groundhog squeezing into a mousehole. Maybe you could pretend there's an elephant standing in the middle of the street?"

"What? And miss the show?" he teased then turned his back out of respect for her pride. She had a lot of it.

Her home was only twenty minutes from Tough's shop, in the wealthy section of town, and they spent most of the ride in silence between her giving him directions.

He pulled up the long, curving drive. A large brick two-story home sat majestically at the top. A massive shiny dark blue and silver motor home, with a BMW SUV attached to it, was parked beside the garage.

"My parents are home," Dusty stated flatly from the back.

Since the only vehicle in sight was the motor home and attached SUV, Roland assumed they must have just arrived in it.

"They've been away?"

"Yeah. They're retired, and they travel the country almost year-round."

He tried to remember her age from her chart. Twenty-six?

Like she could read his mind, or maybe like she'd dealt with these questions all her life, she said, "I have two older brothers. I was an 'oops' that my parents most definitely weren't expecting and didn't really want."

She said it so matter-of-factly, like she really believed it, that Roland was honestly taken aback. His parents weren't the most nurturing people in the world, but he'd never doubted that he'd been wanted.

He glanced in the rearview mirror to see her face, as his heart hurt for her. Maybe this was why she worked so hard to be the best in a sport that wasn't known for its women competitors.

He pulled up beside the RV. "I know you can get out yourself," he started.

Her doorlatch clicking interrupted him. The gentleman in him couldn't let her do it herself. He got out in a hurry.

No question it was awkward, with her back brace and her knee brace, and her shoulder stabilized in a sling. "I can't believe the doctor even lets you out of the house. You're basically a walking medical supply store."

"Funny." She avoided his eyes.

"You're not supposed to be out of the house, are you?" he asked suspiciously, realizing belatedly he should have phrased it as a statement.

"Only for therapy." She hooked a hand over the open door, standing with most of her weight on one foot. "I couldn't stand being cooped up inside all the time." She lifted a shoulder again. "Even when I wasn't racing, Kelly and Cassidy both spend a lot of time helping kids in the area, and Harris has the library, of course, and I was helping one of them constantly on my downtime, but now..." Her fingers tightened, and her eyes closed in frustration. "I'm more helpless than the kids they're working with. I'm pretty much useless."

His hand ached to touch her cheek. He nodded instead. "Yeah, I know. It'd be hard to go from what you were doing to doing nothing."

"Exactly. And when I sit around, all I think about is the stuff I could be doing and the stuff I want to do, and I can't do any of it."

He almost said she should have her friends over, but he'd just seen her friends, and they all had babies and small children. They'd be busy, and Dusty shouldn't be jostled by toddlers and little kids anyway.

"Now that your parents are home, they'll keep you busy."

"They'll be leaving," she said flatly, her expression blank.

It was too much for Roland, and his mouth shot out words faster than his teeth could catch them. "Then I'll come by. I'm not busy tomorrow, and I work early mornings, so I can be here at three o' clock every day. We'll find something to do that won't get you in trouble."

He wasn't skirting the line between therapist and patient any longer. He'd just busted right through it. It was worth it to see how Dusty's face brightened.

But she said, "You don't have to."

"I know. I want to."

Her blue eyes shifted to his, and they stared at each other. Hers wide and uncertain, the most vulnerable he'd seen her. Who knows what she saw on his face? Hopefully the swirling in his chest, that he couldn't even decide what it meant, didn't show up there.

As he looked deeper into her eyes, he had to admit to himself that his feelings really did go beyond the surface therapist-patient relationship.

That thought made him jerk back and look away. He couldn't do that. Not only could he not risk his heart with a woman who raced dirt bikes for fun, but he couldn't risk his job by getting involved with a patient. Just two months ago, his friend and the only other male physical therapist had been fired for getting involved with a patient. Roland knew, with his position as taking on the "tough" cases and also his high-profile clients, that he might be too valuable to get fired, but he didn't want to risk his job. For getting clients in physical therapy, reputation was everything.

Plus, he needed to remember Janice. She was a daredevil, too, although she didn't race.

A little voice in his head reminded him of Dusty's chart. She wouldn't be racing dirt bikes ever again.

He might not lose her like he lost Janice, who loved the speed and thrill of flying. What was wrong with him that he was attracted to daredevil females? Wait. Did he just admit he was attracted to Dusty?

"I want to help." He heard the words come out of his mouth.

She nodded. "Okay. I'd like for you to help me." She looked a little surprised that she said that. He almost laughed at her open mouth and widening eyes. At least he wasn't the only one whose mouth seemed to be running off and leaving the thinking part of their brain far behind.

Her mouth quirked up in a small smile, and his followed. The air between them seemed to swirl, like something fundamental shifted in their relationship.

The spell was broken by a woman's voice calling, "Dusty, honey. Is that you?"

Chapter Seven

Dusty turned, her shaking hand having nothing to do with the pain that throbbed in her back and foot and everything to do with the man standing in front of her. What was that syndrome called? Rescuer syndrome or something? Where one fell in love with one's doctor or nurse or, in her case, therapist.

Great. On top of all her physical problems, now she had mental issues. Just wonderful.

"Hi, Mom." She pasted a smile on her face. Her mom loved her, she was sure of it. But when Dusty was growing up, she didn't really want to be bothered with her, and it was hard to get over that. "Where's Dad?"

"Oh, you know him." Her mom waved her hand. "He has sports on already. We've only been home for five minutes."

Her dad had been a top producer at one of the big sports channels. He'd never been on the air, but he'd lived, breathed, and slept with sports. NASCAR had been his favorite. She had to hand it to her parents; doing the dirt bike circuit when she'd been little hadn't been cheap. They'd never complained one time about the money.

"Come, give me a hug, honey." Her mom wiggled her eyebrows. "And introduce me to your boyfriend." She stopped with her hands on Dusty's shoulders. "You never told me you had a boyfriend."

She shot Roland an apologetic look. "He's not my boyfriend," she said, patting her mom on the back and ignoring the ache in her back at her mom's pressure before letting go. "He's my therapist."

"Oh?" Her mom's voice lowered. "He's a shrink?"

Then he'd *really* be in touch with his feminine side. "No. My physical therapist."

Her mom's brows lowered. "Should he be here? Is that appropriate?"

Her eyes flew to Roland's. Her mom might have been a little put out, raising a child when she wanted to enjoy her late middle age, but she was still very influential in the community, and if she thought there was anything inappropriate going on, Roland could suffer. She didn't want him to lose his job over her with her mom thinking he was here for a social visit. Could she just admit the truth? That Roland had offered her a ride? With only a second to make a decision, she decided not to risk it.

"The doctor said I wasn't supposed to go out, so he's coming here." All technically true.

Her mom looked at the car and the door that was still open. Her brows lowered. "I don't remember seeing that when we pulled in."

"No," Dusty drew the word out. "We were practicing getting in and out." She caught Roland's horrified expression over her mom's shoulder. "And once I was able to get in, I haven't been out in such a long time, I convinced him to give me a ride."

"Well, I do know it gets hard when one has to sit around at home. After I had each of my babies, I got so sick and tired of being home, and that was just a week." She smiled, and Dusty breathed a silent sigh of relief. Roland was off the hook.

"Mom, this is Roland Bryant. Roland, this is my mom, JoAnn." Dusty shut the car door. "I guess we're done with our session?"

"Yes, I'm finished." Roland gave her a look that said he'd be talking to her later. "Do you feel comfortable getting someone to take you to therapy on Monday, or should I come here in the afternoon?"

He asked that for the benefit of her mother, probably. But Dusty hadn't realized that she had a choice.

"You can just come here, Roland," her mom answered for her.

"Dusty always tries to do too much, and I don't want her out before the doctor gives his okay."

Dusty shifted, trying to ease the pain in her back. "I have a doctor appointment on Monday morning. I should know after that if I'm allowed out."

Roland narrowed his eyes at her, concern clouding his face. He'd noticed her discomfort. But he didn't say anything, just nodded.

Then, so her mom would know that there really hadn't been anything inappropriate going on, Dusty fished her phone out of her back pocket, glad she'd worn jeans to the shower because of her braces.

She clicked it on. "Here. How about you put your number in my phone? I'll call you after my appointment and let you know what the doctor says."

Roland took her phone. He looked at it while he spoke to her. "I'll be updated over the computer system, but I'll give you my number anyway, just so you can let me know how you're doing and if you're feeling up to coming into therapy after going to the appointment."

It seemed like he typed a lot longer than he needed to just to put his number in, but Dusty didn't really think about it. She shoved it back in her pocket. "Thanks, Roland. I'll see you Monday."

He gave a small wave. "Monday."

~

AN HOUR LATER, as she was polishing her aluminum bike spokes, Dusty's phone buzzed with a text from Cassidy, wanting to make sure she got home okay. When she went to answer it, she saw what had taken Roland so long to put his number in—he'd typed out a message to her.

> This is the most ingenious way any woman has ever gotten my number.

Dusty grinned. She supposed what she'd done could have been considered hitting on Roland, although she certainly hadn't meant it that way. Had she?

He was attractive, no doubt. With a great personality. He also had compassion and a sense of humor. Any girl would be interested in him, so it wasn't unusual that she had a bit of an interest in the guy.

She rolled her eyes as she rubbed her polishing rag over her bike wheels. She was so full of it. There was no doubt she was attracted to him, and she thought he might feel something too. But he was her therapist. Not to mention she couldn't have a life if she were going after the championship. Some goals left no time for a personal life.

Even as she thought this, her mind was trying to finagle a way to spend more time with him.

～

MONDAY MORNING, Roland had a spring in his step, and his lips kept quirking up. Yesterday had been a long day of doing outside chores around his house. But today he'd see Dusty. He didn't examine his excitement too closely. Of course he liked her. Maybe there was a little attraction there, but he wasn't going to act on it.

The morning flew by.

"I think that Mrs. Stinley has a thing for you." Abigail, one of the other physical therapists, grabbed her salad out of the fridge in the break room.

"She's like eighty." Roland threw his lunch in the microwave and punched some buttons. He really hated it when his coworkers teased him about women crushing on him, since he tried so hard to be professional at all times. Even if the woman in question was elderly.

"She's not dead."

He shrugged, grabbing a water from the fridge. There were usually four therapists on duty and several nurses and office workers. Most of them did errands over lunch and ate out. Roland had a deal worked out with scheduling where he could take a short lunch and leave early. It worked for him, since he needed about five minutes to eat, and that gave him time in the evenings to do what he wanted. Lately, he'd been able to schedule some private consultations.

Eventually, someday, he wanted to open his own practice, focusing on training for injury prevention. There was definitely a market for it, and he'd worked hard for the reputation as the best in his current practice, but to be successful on his own, he needed an even bigger name. For what he wanted to do, it wasn't about saving money to get started, it was about building a reputation. He could be patient. As long as he kept working hard, it would come.

The microwave beeped, and he grabbed his bowl. With his water and spoon in one hand, he started toward the door.

"You know, you could actually sit down and eat," Abigail said from where she sat at the table.

She was new, having only been in the office for a few weeks.

He gave her a smile to ease any sting in his words. "I'm sure you could do what I do—give up the lunch break and get out early." Actually, he was sure she could. Lunchtime was one of their busiest times of day. People wanted to schedule their therapy so they didn't miss work. Legally, the company couldn't make them work through their lunch, but they could volunteer.

Abigail shrugged dismissively. "They offered to let me do that when they hired me, but I can't go all day without eating, and I can't eat a salad in five minutes."

Roland jerked his head in acknowledgment and walked out of the lunchroom to the high desk, which was now deserted, that held the computers they used to type up their notes and get the doctors' information on patients.

He'd been eager—too eager—all day to see how Dusty's appointment went.

Punching in the password and pulling up the screen he wanted, Roland waited, chewing. Finally the info he needed loaded, and he took another bite as he read through the notes.

She'd not been given permission to lose the brace nor to drive. Basically the doctor had noted that she was "making progress" but was still in pain and needed to rest, other than therapy.

Dusty had cancelled her afternoon appointment. The doctor also had a note that the patient was doing "at-home" therapy with the same therapy group she'd been seeing.

So she was going to hold him to going to her house. One part of him thrilled at that. The other part wished he'd never suggested it.

They didn't need any special equipment, since, unless it was absolutely necessary, he always tried to plan a patient's program so they could do it at home without a big, expensive purchase. It wasn't that.

He already had a hard time keeping her off his mind. Saturday, it had been too tempting to run his fingers through her hair and see if it was as soft as it looked. Not to mention his odd desire to touch her, and not in a clinical way. He couldn't allow himself to cross that line. Especially if he intended to start his own practice. Patients needed to be able to trust their therapist.

As he finished his lunch, he ran down through his afternoon appointments. Nothing difficult.

The hours dragged, and he was uncharacteristically distracted as he finished out his day. Normally he loved helping people find ways to deal with the pain and get their range of motion and motor abilities back. Hard, but rewarding.

He gave his last patient their instructions and made sure they had a ride before grabbing his things, saying farewell to his coworkers, and heading out the back door.

His phone buzzed just as he was stepping out.

It wasn't a number he recognized, but he smiled as he read the message.

> When you can barely move, you have to get creative.

He actually laughed out loud as he clicked the fob in his hand. She'd gotten his message anyway.

> What time do you want me?

He hit send before he got in and started the car.

> Come at four. You can stay for dinner.

That was tempting. He'd really like to get to know Dusty outside of therapy. Normally, he'd feel like as long as they weren't actually doing therapy sessions, it would be okay for them to develop a friendship. He considered a lot of his clients friends. But with this attraction he felt, could he keep her at a friend's level?

Everything in him wanted to try. Aside from the attraction he felt, Dusty was a nice person, who could really use a friend right now. One who didn't have small children and a spouse demanding their time.

To give himself some time to think, he typed,

What's on the menu?

Idk. I'd have to ask the housekeeper.

Tempted to accept, Roland forced himself to type out,

Not today. Maybe some other time.

He couldn't quite get himself to turn her down flat. Because he really wanted to eat with her. But housekeeper?

He grunted. Maybe because she raced motocross, or maybe because she was just so unpretentious, but it had really surprised him to find that Dusty's family was so wealthy. He wasn't exactly slouching in his current job, and he had plans to go even bigger, but they had a wealth he definitely wasn't used to. Who had a housekeeper?

Dusty, apparently.

Were her parents still home? He supposed he'd find out at four. That was another thing he'd found really hard to believe. How could a parent—a mother, especially—have her daughter go through all this therapy by herself and not feel the need to be with her, helping? It'd be one thing if she had a job and couldn't. But to leave her child alone so she could travel in her RV... No wonder Dusty was so determined to excel in a dangerous, male-dominated sport.

He rang her bell right at four, after a short debate with himself about whether to go to the front door or the back door. When he'd been there Friday, they'd disappeared around the back of the house, so he assumed the family used the back door.

He'd settled on the front door. He'd like to be friends with Dusty, but he was there in a professional capacity, so that's how he was going to play it.

The RV was no longer in the drive, but maybe it was out for maintenance? He could hardly believe that her parents would have left again already. Dusty was a grown adult, but still...

A woman in shorts and a t-shirt, with a bandana tied around her hair and her eyes smiling, answered the door, holding it open but not inviting him in. "Hello."

"I'm Roland Bryant, the therapist."

The woman stepped back. "Dusty said it was probably you. Come on in." She closed the door behind him. "Follow me."

He managed to keep his mouth closed as he looked around at the immaculate tile floors and soaring ceilings. The house was bigger than it looked from the outside, and he wasn't entirely sure he could find his way out as the housekeeper took him back a short hall and down some steps.

Dusty waited at the bottom. "Thanks, Blanche."

Blanche stood aside and waited for him to pass before heading back up the steps.

"I would have answered the door myself, but..." Dusty shrugged, indicating her braced leg.

"It's fine," he said. Her blond hair was pulled back in its typical ponytail and hung over her shoulder down past her stomach. He shoved back the urge to see it down. She wore yoga pants and a t-shirt. He saw outfits like that a thousand times a day, and his heart never did the strange thumping it was doing in his chest now.

If she had makeup on, he couldn't tell. She looked fresh and happy, and so beautiful she made his eyes hurt, especially when she turned the wattage of her smile directly onto him. He figured he could safely assume that the doctor hadn't told her she'd never race again.

"Your parents have left again?" he asked, breaking the silence.

She blinked, looking away, and he wished he hadn't asked.

"There's a race in Kansas."

"NASCAR?"

"Yep."

"I thought the races were on Sundays." He didn't follow motor sports at all, but he did watch sports channels and knew a little.

"Dad likes to get a good spot." She shrugged. "There are a bunch of people who have RVs and follow the races. They all know each other, and they hang out together."

Her parents left her to go "hang out" with their friends. Anger flared in his chest. He reminded himself she wasn't a child. He supposed she was lucky they let her live with them. Which maybe was why the next question tumbled off his tongue without thought.

"Do you do anything? I mean, besides race?"

She gave him an assessing glance, like she was trying to figure out why he asked.

"I have a graphic design degree. I pick up freelance work on the internet." She gave a humorless laugh. "I've been doing a lot of it lately."

"I see."

She moved into the room and spread her hand around. A wet bar lined one wall. There was a treadmill and a few other exercise-type pieces of equipment grouped along the far wall. A cluster of couches and recliners circled a gas fireplace and a big-screen TV hung on the wall above it. A few magazines lay on the coffee table. The walls gleamed white, and even though it was a basement area, it felt spacious and open.

"Where do you want to work?"

If he didn't know better, he'd almost say she was nervous. She twisted her fingers and didn't meet his eyes again. Was he having that effect on her? Maybe she was worried about what he'd think of her home? He couldn't think of another reason for her to be shifting her feet and twining the ends of her ponytail.

"Is everything okay?" he asked, unable to ignore the fact that there might be something wrong.

Her head jerked, and her eyes widened. "Uh, yeah. Yes." She laughed. "Okay. I'm sorry. It just feels a little weird having you in my home...doing this here."

He smiled. He wasn't sure, but he thought that meant it actually was him that was making her nervous.

"Well, let's just get started, then, okay? Take your brace off, and we'll go to the steps first."

He set his briefcase down on the counter and pulled out her chart. One of the benefits of working in the center was the computer access. He had the internet. That was it.

"You'll have to tell the doctor that you're seeing me personally, if that's what you want." He looked over his shoulder. "Our office doesn't actually do outpatient, but I'm set up with my own business and license. The doctor just has to know and approve, and you'll have to notify your insurance." He had done this a few times with different patients. Not very often. Technically, there was a clause in his contract to the effect that he wouldn't steal clients from the practice, but they'd allowed him to give home therapy sessions to already participating clients if coming to the center was too much for them. Eventually, Roland knew the center he worked for wanted to add home visits, but they didn't have the structure in place to do so as of yet.

She nodded as she set her bulky knee brace aside. She still didn't seem completely comfortable, so he figured it was his job to make things "normal."

"Ready? Let's get to work."

She stood. He gave her his elbow and a dark look when she acted like she wasn't going to take it.

"Did you recover from Saturday? Still sore? How's your back?"

He fired the questions off in his most professional tone. Maybe they were both attracted to each other. Whatever kinds of complicated that made their relationship, he wasn't going to let it get in the way of giving her the best therapy he could.

Chapter Eight

All week, Dusty worked her butt off for Roland. She loved doing the therapy in her home. It kept her from feeling like she was bothering her friends.

By the next Monday, things had relaxed between them to the point where she'd gotten Roland to agree to stay for dinner. A win.

They started therapy at four as usual. An hour later, they were both sweating. Dusty swiped a hand over her forehead. Not that the therapy was so hard but pushing through the pain did take a toll. Her home was warmer than the therapy center, too.

Roland always took charge and acted like everything was completely normal, which made things so much easier for her. He also dressed more casually for her home therapy. He'd come in jeans and a t-shirt. He looked way too much like he did after the shower when she'd wanted to walk into his arms and run her hands down his back. Not the kind of thoughts she should be having about her therapist.

But he'd been nothing but professional, which was a little disappointing, if she were to be honest.

He reached around, pointing to his back. "These are the muscles that should feel the pull."

"They hurt," she said bluntly.

He laughed. "Muscle pain is better than pain in your spine." He tilted his head. "Which is not hurting, correct?"

She scrunched her nose up. Pain was pretty much a part of her life; she didn't always try to figure out where it was coming from. "I don't think so."

"Mind if I run my fingers down your spine?"

Her shoulder lifted. "Go ahead."

He did so, and his touch was clinical, his expression professional, his stance appropriate. Her mind knew it, but her body still buzzed at his nearness. The scent of his cologne wafted by, just strong enough to fill her lungs and flip her heart.

She set her jaw. "I still have a backbone?"

"Yep."

"Then you and the doctor I saw this morning agree on something."

"I agree with everything he's said so far."

She dropped her hands and turned. Her back protested with a sharp pang, and she flinched. "Even with my not driving?"

"Yes. Even with you not driving. Your body is healing quickly, but you're still not nearly as strong as you were. With the pain, your reaction time is slowed, and you shouldn't be jerking yourself around. It wouldn't take much to undo everything you've done to recover. Plus, your spine is still hurting you, and you want that to heal right."

"Yeah. If I'm going to race again, it needs to be right."

He blinked, then he looked away, his mouth flat.

"What?" she asked.

"You'll need to talk to your doctor about that."

"About what?"

"About racing again."

"You mean, about *when* I can race again."

He shrugged. Then his face resumed the professional mask he wore during their sessions. "I have one more exercise I'd like to show you. I think you're ready. You flinched a little when I ran my fingers over your spine, but some of that was anticipating the pain."

"It didn't hurt that much," she said, eager to move on.

The doorbell rang.

Who could that be? Dusty looked toward the stairs. Blanche would get it. Normally she'd run upstairs, hollering, "I've got it!" But she wasn't running anywhere.

"You need to go?" Roland asked.

"No. If it's someone for me, Blanche will bring them down."

"Okay. So, you need to put your feet shoulder width apart, no farther." He demonstrated with his own feet and nodded in approval while she imitated him.

"That's good. Now, I want you to push out with your knees..."

"Dusty! What are you doing down here..." Kelly appeared on the stairs. "Oh, I'm sorry. I didn't mean to interrupt."

Dusty straightened. "Hey, no problem. Come on down. You know Roland."

"Good to see you, Kelly," Roland said. "How'd you get away without the kids?"

"Tough had a light afternoon, and he quit early. He's actually in the car with the kids, and we were taking them out, but Cassidy texted me asking if I was taking you to therapy, because Riley had told her that she wasn't."

"She hasn't had her baby, yet?"

"Not yet." Kelly smiled. "Any second now."

"Can't be soon enough for her, I'm sure."

"Nope. Anyway, she had asked Eden and Eve if they were taking you." Dusty nodded. Eden and Eve Baxter were the twin sisters of the Baxter boys. They had both taken her to therapy, and they'd taken turns staying with her after her accident along with their sisters-in-law. They didn't have children, and they'd often taken the night shift.

"But Eden and Eve said they weren't, and," Kelly glanced at Roland, "long story short, we figured out no one was taking you to therapy. There's so many of us that we all just assumed someone else was doing it. Then we realized no one did it last week at all. You haven't been answering your phone..." Kelly's brows slid up.

Dusty lifted a hand. "Sorry! It's over there on the bar. We've been working for almost an hour."

Kelly shook her head. "It's okay. It's just not like you to ignore your phone, so since I was going out, I said we'd stop by." She paused and gave Roland a thoughtful look. "This means you're not doing therapy at the center anymore?"

"No." Dusty didn't know what that look from Kelly meant, but Roland wasn't getting in trouble for this. "I'm sorry. I should have called, but I've had a big design project I've been working on, and I didn't. It's a pain for everyone to have to take me—"

"It is not!" Kelly interrupted. She finished coming down the stairs and practically marched over to Dusty. "We love you." She wrapped her arms around Dusty, knowledgeable enough about her injuries that she didn't squeeze. "We want to take you. And we were really worried about you when we realized we didn't know what was going on with you. With so many people involved, it gets a little dicey."

Their concern touched her heart. Warmth flooded her chest, and tears pricked her eyes. Her parents had left today with barely a hug. Of course she was twenty-six and a responsible adult, but their complete lack of concern still hurt. She bit her lip. Out of the corner of her eye, she realized Roland had not missed any of that and watched her face intently, with an inscrutable expression on his.

"Thank you," Dusty whispered in Kelly's ear, blinking back the tears.

"We love you," Kelly whispered back. "I love you," she added as though Dusty might not have understood.

"I love you too, and I owe you all so much for everything you've done."

"That's bologna," Kelly said, stepping back but keeping her hands on Dusty's shoulders. "If you weren't at a race or practice, you've been there every single time we've had any kind of work day or fundraiser, and how many times have you watched our children for us, and been the errand runner, since it's so much easier for you when you don't have little ones to get in and out...don't even get me started," Kelly said with a laugh.

"Thanks." Dusty smiled. "And thanks for checking on me. I'm fine, and Tough's waiting in the car."

"That's the nice thing about a husband who doesn't talk much. He's definitely not going to yell at me when I get back out to the car, no matter how long it takes."

"Maybe he'll drive off without you."

Kelly laughed and turned toward the stairs. "Now, that's a distinct possibility."

Dusty knew it was no such thing. Tough probably didn't shower Kelly with fancy love words, but it would be hard to find a man more devoted to his wife. Dusty could only hope she'd find a guy who treated her as well.

As Kelly disappeared up the stairs, she called back down, "Someone will be around to visit tomorrow."

"You don't have to do that," Dusty called back.

"We want to."

Dusty sighed and looked around. Sometime after she'd met his eyes, Roland had moved away and now stood at the bar, typing something into his computer. He looked up, his face a question.

"Sorry about that." Dusty started to limp over.

"Having a great support system in place will do more than physical therapy to help you get better."

"Really? You're admitting therapy doesn't solve the world's problems?"

"Not even close." He walked slowly over. "This isn't the most professional thing I've ever said, but it bothers me how little your parents seem to care." His eyes gazed down into hers, and she again needed to blink back tears. She was never tempted to cry. It must be hormones.

"I appreciate you saying so. It definitely hurts, but I'm used to it. I've never been a top priority for them." She fingered her hair. His eyes seemed drawn to it.

Then his lip drew back, and he looked away. "You ready to finish? I'd really like to show you this one last exercise."

She nodded, and they went back to their positions. He corrected her posture, but again, he was the ultimate professional, like his little confession about her parents had never happened. Like he put the walls up between them again.

Having Kelly there had gotten Dusty to thinking, not that she hadn't already spent a pile of time thinking about Roland. He'd be a great guy. Whatever girl ended up with him would be one lucky woman.

Why didn't he have a girl? The thought stopped her cold.

"You okay?" he immediately asked, concern etched in every line and feature.

"Fine." She brushed off his concern, concentrating on doing her exercise correctly. She wanted to race. Not get married.

"I think that's enough for today." Roland straightened and put his hands on his hips. "You'll need to do these tomorrow morning. We'll see how you're doing tomorrow afternoon, then. Any questions?" He waited for her head shake then helped her to the chair where her braces were. While she put them on, he walked over and opened his laptop, punching the keys and clicking through pages.

"Is it a problem doing the therapy here?" she asked.

She loved her friends, and it felt amazingly good that Kelly had stopped to check on her, but she loved being independent. After so many years of fending for herself, it was hard to depend completely on other people. Especially when they were so busy. She supposed if they lived in a larger city, there would be more options for transportation, but even Uber didn't pick up here.

He didn't look up and continued typing. "Nope. It's actually better for me."

After fixing the last strap in place, she struggled to her feet. He had closed his laptop and stood with his arms crossed and one hip leaning against the counter.

Conscious that he was staying for dinner for the first time, she said, "I'd ask if you'd be okay while I took a quick shower, but with these," she indicated her braces, "nothing is quick."

One side of his mouth quirked up. "Take a shower. I can entertain myself."

"Come on upstairs. You can hang out in the living room. Blanche will have dinner ready at six."

He still had that distance, like he was deliberating keeping walls between them. It was for the best, she supposed, but she wished their easy camaraderie was back. No. What she really missed was the heat in his gaze the few times his professional shell had slipped.

She showered as fast as she could, but it was still thirty minutes before she was back out in the living room. Roland stood in front of the big floor-to-ceiling window with his hands in his pockets, staring outside.

If he heard her approach, he didn't let on, and she admired his strong jaw, the way his muscles bunched under his t-shirt, and the image of relaxed power he presented.

Not only would he treat his woman right, she'd have a feast for her eyes every day. Dusty would not allow herself to be jealous of a woman she didn't even know existed.

"Why don't you have a girlfriend?" She wanted to slap her hand over her mouth as soon as the sentence was out. She could blame her braces for making her reactions slow.

His head jerked around. His brows lowered while his mouth opened in surprise. After a second, his body turned more fully. "I'm sorry. I didn't hear you come in."

The question was out there. Should she demand an answer? Obviously, he didn't want to address it.

But she hadn't gotten to the top of the elite group of the motocross world by not taking risks. "That wasn't an answer." She walked into the room and leaned against the back of the couch.

"I had one once. Sometimes once is enough."

A cryptic answer that didn't really answer anything. She allowed her expression to let him know what she thought of his non-answer.

"I'm not asking you about boyfriends. Is someone going to come home and challenge me to a duel?" His eyes shifted. "Or is he still out on the circuit while you recoup at home?"

"I'm too competitive for me to see another racer as anything other than a competitor. Someone to beat. I have a few guys I practice with, and I might call them friends on a good day. They treat me like a boy." She shrugged. "I look like one with my helmet on. I'm not trying to distract them or use my feminine wiles to get ahead. I want to succeed because I'm the best. Not because some guy lost his head over a pretty face."

Roland nodded slowly like he understood. Dusty wasn't even sure most women understood. It was so ingrained in the female psyche to use their looks and their figure to sway a man's agenda, and it was so ingrained in a man to defer to someone he'd been taught was weaker and needed protection.

Physically, yeah, she'd never be as strong as even an average man, but mentally, she was as tough as an Antarctic winter. Races were won with mental toughness.

But if she won because some man gave quarter to her, because that's what he'd been trained to do, then the win wasn't fair, and she didn't want it. She didn't want a spot, a win, a prize, anything, because she was a woman. She only wanted what she earned straight up.

"So…" He drew the word out, like he knew he'd hit one of her buttons. "We can agree that you're pretty?"

She laughed, all her righteous anger over being catered to because she was a woman evaporating with his silly question.

"Nope." She crossed her arms over her chest and tried to hide her grin. "I'm in fighting mode now, and I won't agree with anything you say."

Immediately his face changed, like she'd challenged him. He took a step toward her. Then another. "Really? You won't agree with anything?"

She felt like he was stalking her as he moved closer. Slowly. It was exactly what she'd been wanting from him—for him to drop the professional cover.

Resisting the urge to back up, she kept her arms crossed and reminded herself that she didn't back down from a challenge.

A little smile played around his lips, and he leaned closer. "You're not agreeing with anything I say?" he asked again, but it felt like a reminder.

She shook her head.

He brought one hand up. His fingers closed carefully around the still slightly damp hair that lay over her shoulder in its typical ponytail. His eyes held hers.

"There's no reason why I shouldn't kiss you right now," he said, his voice rough and low.

She'd faced down dirt tracks, powerful motors about to be unleashed rumbling beside her and under her, death a split-second mistake from claiming a young victim, and her insides had not rioted like they did with his one simple statement.

She was supposed to do something. She couldn't remember what.

Her hand somehow landed on his chest, and the heat burned through her fingers and up her arm. His breath mingled with hers, and she leaned forward, knowing she shouldn't but unable to remember why.

He leaned closer. She raised her head.

"Fight me, Dusty," he whispered.

But she couldn't remember why she should, why she was going to. And she didn't want to anyway.

His lips hovered over hers, their eyes still connected. She was frozen. Couldn't move, and didn't want to, unless it was to get closer.

He broke the spell with a tug on her hair. His finger came up, and he brushed her cheek with the back of it, sending a thrill down her spine. He swallowed and straightened.

She let out a shaky breath.

"So we found something else we agree on?" he asked, his voice not sounding quite normal, either.

"No," she said, not sure if she was saying she thought he should or shouldn't kiss her, just remembering she'd promised to disagree then promptly fell right under his spell. He didn't do it to women all the time, she was sure of it. But he was amazingly good at making a girl forget her name. Talk about not playing fair. She'd been so upset about women using their feminine wiles. That was nothing to when Roland used his manly charm. She hadn't thought she was so susceptible.

"Dinner's ready." Blanche spoke from the edge of the living room, poking her head in the doorway.

There was a respectable distance between them—she was at the back of the couch; he stood at the side. Neither of them jumped. Not that Blanche would say anything.

"We're coming. Thank you." Dusty moved. Waiting until Blanche's footsteps faded away, Dusty said, "That was about two minutes of forgetting I'm in constant pain. Thank you."

"So, we agree that I make a great distraction, too?" he said with a smile that didn't quite reach his eyes. She got the feeling he was annoyed, but at himself, not her.

"You're determined that we need to agree, aren't you?"

"You think you have the corner on stubbornness and competitiveness?"

"Stubborn? That doesn't sound very nice."

"It's a weakness that can be a strength if you use it right." He walked around the couch. "I don't know what she made, but it smells good."

"Blanche is a great cook." Dusty finally felt like her heart had settled down, and she could finally breathe without gasping. Was he right about her stubbornness? She'd never considered that anything but a liability. "I suppose the positive side of stubbornness is determination."

"Or perseverance," he said easily. He kept a distance between them again, and it irritated her. How could he blow so hot one minute and act like they were just distant friends the next?

Well, she didn't need to be affected by their encounter either. If he wanted distant friends, she could do that.

Chapter Nine

All week, Roland continued to go to Dusty's house after work and do her therapy session there. But he didn't stay for dinner again. He spent the entire night Monday night castigating himself for diving across that therapist-client line. He had come dangerously close to crossing his own standards, not to mention conventional health care standards.

The thing was, half the time he was wondering why he didn't just kiss her. She obviously wasn't telling him no. He couldn't even get her to fight him if he begged.

That was easy on the ego.

Or maybe she was just so surprised that her therapist would be so unprofessional. She didn't say. But it was impossible now for him to do therapy with her and not notice her wild and determined scent. It held just a hint of fruit and all of Dusty. He craved it more than coffee.

Or her hair, which he'd loved from the first but had to fist his hand to keep from running his fingers through it.

Or her...

He shook his head. He had to stop thinking about her.

He tried to focus on finishing the last patient's notes. It was Friday, and after he went to Dusty's and gave her the last session for the week, he would find something to do to take his mind off a certain blue-eyed blond.

He clicked out of the computer program.

"Hey, Roland." Abigail stood on the other side of the high counter, her hand on a patient's folder.

Jerking his head at her, he said, "Abigail." Gathering his folder, he placed it on the pile to be filed.

When he looked up, Abigail was still in the same spot, still looking at him.

"I have two tickets to the doubleheader baseball game tomorrow." She gave him a sweet smile. "Are you interested?" She held up a hand. "Just a friends thing. I'm not trying to start an office romance." She fake shuddered. "That would be awkward."

Yeah. Not quite as awkward as obsessing over his patient. But still awkward.

But here was the distraction he needed. Getting out of the house. A good ball game. Abigail would be decent company.

Yeah, this was exactly what he needed.

"Thanks for thinking of me, but I can't. I, uh…" And he couldn't think of an excuse. The silence became awkward.

Finally her sweet smile became an annoyed frown. "You just don't want to go with me."

He sighed and let his head fall forward. "If I accepted, it's because I have someone else on my mind, and I'd only be using you as a distraction." There. He liked honesty, but that might have been a little too brutally honest.

But Abigail nodded. "I appreciate you being straight with me." Her lips curved back up a little. "We really could go just as friends."

It still didn't sit right. He shook his head. "Thanks anyway."

"Enjoy your weekend," she said as she grabbed the next folder and walked away.

"You too."

On his way out to his car, his phone buzzed with a text.

> Eat with me tonight?

Dusty.

He wanted to say yes. Just three letters. His thumbs hovered over the keypad. But his career loomed large behind him. Could he eat with her again? Spend an evening sparring with her? Laughing with her? Admiring her? And not cross that line?

Probably not.

He forced his thumbs to move.

Not tonight.

When he arrived at her house, Blanche let him in. They'd been doing this enough that he walked himself down the stairs.

Dusty was ready with her brace off, sitting on the barstool, looking at her phone.

"Hey, you made it." She smiled, but her cheerfulness seemed forced.

His was definitely fake. "You ready? Let's do this."

Their whole session was like that, each of them pretending to be happy, neither of them actually feeling it.

Finally they finished up the last exercise, and she moved to put her brace back on.

Rather than go over to his computer, he moved over beside her. She ignored him. Like she didn't know he was there.

"Dusty?"

"Yeah," she said, bending over, fumbling with the brace that she could put on and off in her sleep.

"I can't eat with you and keep the professional distance that needs to be between us."

"Whatever." Dusty kept her head down.

He hunkered down and placed his hands over hers. They were soft and warm, and he wanted to slide his hands over her skin, linking their fingers together. He didn't.

She pulled her hands away and started working on her brace again.

"Listen to me, please," he said softly.

"I heard you. You don't want to stay. Some professional crap. Whatever. It's fine." She emphasized the last statement with a last tug at her brace and pushed herself up.

He almost fell backward getting out of her way.

"I'm serious."

"Me too. I decided I'm going out tonight anyway." She looked him in the eye with a shrug and a smile that didn't make it to her eyes. "I need to get ready. We're done here."

"You're not allowed to drive."

"What's the doctor going to do? Call the police? They can arrest me. That's fine. I'm sick of sitting around, and I'm not doing it tonight." She crossed her arms over her chest. "Actually, never mind. You're the professional, and I'm just the lowly person, same as every other lowly person you work with all day long. It violates our professional relationship for me to even tell you this. Forget I said anything. You don't need to know what I'm doing tonight or any other night—"

She stopped abruptly as he stepped close and gripped her fists. "Stop. I care about you, Dusty. Too much." Her eyes snapped to his. They narrowed as though reading his mind, checking it out, and making sure he was being honest.

He couldn't stand being so near to her and not touching her. He dropped one of her hands to cup her cheek. "It kills me to walk out every day, thinking about you here, alone, and me going home, alone, and how much better it would be for us to be together."

"Then why not stay?"

His throat closed, and he tried to speak around the big knot in it. "I don't think I can be just friends with you."

"Then don't be just friends."

He looked away. "I can't be more."

"I'll find another therapist."

He jerked his head back. She shifted her hand, and he realized he was squeezing her fist painfully.

His chest constricted, and he couldn't breathe. "No."

"It's the perfect solution."

"I don't trust anyone else to give you the best care possible." All the nights he couldn't sleep, he spent up searching for exercises for Dusty's specific injuries. Reading case studies about what had worked and what didn't. He could recite many of them from memory. No one else would put that kind of time into her recovery. She might never walk without a limp again. She might always have back pain. She might never regain full motion in her shoulder, but it wouldn't be because her therapist hadn't turned over every stone, hadn't used only the best techniques, hadn't spent hours researching and sorting and analyzing the data.

"That's my decision," she said softly.

He shook his head. "It doesn't matter." He hesitated. "Sit down for a minute."

Dusty never questioned him when he told her what to do with her therapy, so he was a little surprised when she resisted the pressure of his hand that still held her balled fist.

"What? Is this something so bad I need to sit down?"

"I need to sit."

"Oh." Her face softened. "Okay."

He dropped her fist, and they went over to the bar where his computer sat. She adjusted the stool and sat. He sat at the end, somewhat facing her. Then he popped back up. He hadn't told this story since it happened. His parents knew some. His brother much less. But for some reason, he felt like he needed to tell Dusty everything.

"I was engaged once."

Her mouth opened then closed. "I think you mentioned a fiancée once."

"Her name was Janice."

"That's right. You...you talk about her in past tense. What happened?" Her fingers fiddled with her ponytail.

Before he could begin, a voice came down the stairs. "Where's my little sis?" A tall man with blond hair who looked to be around fifty appeared. He was trailed by a young man with hair a shade darker.

Dusty stiffened then stood. "Max. Tucker." She smiled, but it was her fake smile, and got up. Roland watched as Dusty walked over, trying her best not to limp. If he hadn't spent so much time with her, he might not have noticed, but it was obvious to him that she was trying to hide her weakness.

"Max, this is Roland, my physical therapist."

"Your therapist?" Max's blue eyes narrowed, his crow's feet fanning out on both temples. "You guys were a little cozy for a therapist, don't you think?"

Roland slanted Dusty a I-told-you-so look, which she ignored. He stepped forward. "We were done with the session, and I was just leaving." He held his hand out. "Good to see Dusty has some family around."

"This is my nephew Tucker." She indicated the boy, and her fond smile was real. "Tucker, meet Roland."

Max and Tucker both shook his hand. Roland was impressed with the boy's firm grip and how he met his eye. He was tall, like his dad, his shoulders showed the promise of width, and his eyes were intelligent and kind. Roland immediately liked him. He didn't get the same feeling about Max.

"Well, little sis, I guess we came at a good time, then. Since the therapy guy is heading out." Max laughed like he'd said something funny.

Dusty shifted uncomfortably. This was her brother and nephew. It was okay for Roland to leave her alone with them, right?

He tried to meet Dusty's eye, but she gave him her fake smile. "I'll need to let Blanche know if you're staying for supper."

"Blanche is still here?" Max said with surprise. "I can't get any housekeeper to stay more than a month or two. How about it, Tucker?" He laughed again. Roland figured he must be one of those people who laughed after everything he said. As in, "My dog died." Big laugh. "Saturn has rings." Big laugh. "I haven't been in to see my sister since she was almost killed in a motocross accident." Big laugh.

Roland shook his head and headed toward the door.

"Thanks," Dusty said behind him.

He turned. Was she being sarcastic?

He was behind Max who was telling Dusty about the traffic they'd run into on the way there. Meeting Dusty's eyes behind Max's shoulder, he mouthed, *Do you want me to stay?*

Her nod was almost imperceptible.

Okay, he mouthed back.

She brightened immediately. "Oh, Roland. You know, you could stay too. Max has so many fascinating stories from the time he spent in China."

Max turned. "That's true. China is wide open for investment if you know how to work around their government." He laughed. "They're cheap as all get-out, and the person who can cut the most corners wins." He laughed again. "You just don't want to use their subway. Never know when the thing is going to collapse." He laughed. "Same with skyscrapers. Couldn't pay me to go in one of those." He laughed. "Yep. Basically, there aren't any safety standards. Which makes the red tape easy." Yep, he laughed again, and Roland figured this was going to be one long night.

~

DUSTY CHEWED HER FOOD, whatever it was, she couldn't taste it, and tried to keep a pleasant expression on her face. For Tucker's sake.

Max laughed again, and she tried to turn her grimace into a smile. Across the table from her, Roland seemed to be occupied with the same struggle. Her smile became real as she stifled a laugh at the contortions the corner of his mouth went through. Down, up, down, up, twist back, flatten, up. There. It was up. Wait. Back down. She giggled.

His eyes snapped to hers. Immediately she shoved another spoonful of food into her mouth.

"And that's why I left China, never to return." Max laughed before reaching for his wineglass.

Dusty took a sip of her water. At least having Max here interrupted the doldrum of her day.

"I see," Roland said. Although Dusty was pretty sure he didn't see at all. He had been so busy trying to make himself smile, he couldn't possibly have been paying attention. "Tucker. Have you been spending all these years in China, too?"

"No—"

"Glad you mentioned him. He's the reason we're here." Max laughed.

Dusty cringed.

"You're going to that race tomorrow, aren't you?"

Roland's water glass hung suspended in midair. His eyes met Dusty's. It felt like guilt oozed out of every pore. She dropped her gaze before straightening her shoulders and lifting her chin.

Before she could open her mouth, Roland said, "She's going with me."

She barely contained her relief behind a cool smile. "Yes. Roland is taking me to the race tomorrow. Nice, isn't it?"

"Therapist, my foot," Max muttered.

Dusty was so relieved he didn't laugh that she almost laughed. She stopped herself just in time. After a few days with Max, it took her a month to laugh without self-consciousness again.

"Dusty is still not steady on her feet, but of course she couldn't miss the race. She's paying me to accompany her," Roland said, his face a mask of innocence.

Dusty was so relieved, she figured she really would pay him.

"Great. Great." Max laughed. "Tucker has been asking to go for a long time. Several years. But those track grandstands are hotbeds of germs and diseases, and his mother wouldn't even consider going with him. So, I decided he could go with you." He laughed.

Dusty stared at him, her food forgotten. "You want me to take him?" she asked, thankful that was the question that came out of her mouth and not, "Why would a twenty-something-year-old man need me to take him to a motocross race?"

Max looked at her like she'd just asked him if the ocean was wet. "Of course. When we go somewhere, we don't go as plebeian spectators. We meet the important people." He laughed. "The people with money, of course." He laughed again, but his blue eyes never left Dusty's face. "I assumed, since our parents made sure I understood how good you were at the bike racing, that you know the people he needs to be introduced to." He laughed. "Don't waste his time with anyone else."

"I actually just wanted to watch the—"

Like his son hadn't spoken, Max said, "I'm not going. I'm getting a massage and meeting friends of mine for a vineyard tour and wine tasting." He laughed. "I'll be back late—don't wait up—and we'll leave after brunch Sunday morning."

He put his spoon down and drank the rest of his wine. He looked around. "Where's Blanche? Someone needs to tell that woman how to buy good wine." He laughed and poured himself another glass.

Dusty noticed that Roland was finished eating. At least she could get him out of here. She tapped her napkin to her lips then set it down. "If you'll excuse us, Roland had something he needed to do tonight."

"That's fine. See you later, Roland." Max's laugh grated on Dusty's last nerve. Her hand fisted in her lap.

"I need your help," Roland said, and Dusty managed to keep herself from leaping over the table and kissing him by the barest fraction of self-control.

"Of course. You don't mind, right, Max?" The tone of her voice held relief. Max would probably not notice.

"Nope, not at all. Tucker and I are going to watch the game." He looked around. "Where's your TV?" He laughed. "Blanche better have the bar stocked."

Dusty didn't know or care. She was up before he had the statement out of his mouth. Her eye caught on Tucker, and a small amount of pity popped in her chest. But it was soon gone. He was a man, old enough to stand up for himself. Which is what he needed to do if he were ever going to get out from under Max's command. Even as she thought that, though, she respected a son who honored his father. Even if that father was as annoying as Max.

Tucker watched her with the blue eyes of his dad. She gave a little shrug. "I'll let you know what time we're leaving tomorrow."

He nodded. Really, Tucker seemed like a decent guy. He was her nephew, but since they lived so far away, she'd never really gotten to know him. Maybe tomorrow would be her chance.

Chapter Ten

Roland followed Dusty out of the kitchen, Max's laugh ringing in his ear. "Man, I feel bad for his wife," he said softly over Dusty's shoulder.

She opened the front door. "They're divorced."

Roland didn't say the sarcastic comment that came to his mind. The guy was Dusty's brother. He walked through the front door, closing it behind him. "He seems like an okay guy."

Dusty lifted a shoulder. "He is. Harmless."

"Is this the first time he's been here since your accident?"

"Yep." Dusty stopped at the bottom of the steps and stood on the walk.

Roland bit his tongue again. If Dusty were his sister, he'd have been by her side the entire time. He wasn't close to his brother, but if his brother had an accident, Roland would at least have visited and checked to see if there was anything he could do.

He tried to shove aside the anger at Max for being a selfish bore. After all, her parents didn't care either. It must run in the family.

"What about your other brother?"

"Mitchel is a year younger than Max. He's married with two girls."

She gave him an apologetic look. "I really don't know them that well. They were both in college when I was born."

Dusty stood before him, so sweet and vulnerable. Tough and strong, of course, but hurting because her family didn't really seem to care about her. If only he could fix all the things that were wrong in her life. Give her a family that cared. Give her everything she wanted. But Roland knew he wouldn't really be doing her a favor. If he took away the struggle, the victory wasn't as sweet.

Still, something inside of him longed to hold and comfort her. He stepped a little closer to her and put his hand on her cheek, before he remembered that he was her therapist and Max already thought their relationship was too close. Exactly what Roland had feared.

He dropped his hand. "I didn't realize there was a race tomorrow."

"Yeah, it's not too far away in Dry Run."

"Were you planning on going?" His heart hurt a little to think that she hadn't mentioned it to him. Not that she needed to or anything.

"No. I wasn't." Her mouth quirked up. "I guess I am, now." Her face brightened into a full-on smile. "It's easier to just go along with Max than fight him sometimes."

"Do you mind if I go, too?" Spending time with her would be fun. He'd also never seen a motocross race. Plus, he figured if he went, she would have less chance of overdoing it.

If possible, her smile widened. "I'd love that."

They stared at each other. He shoved his hand in his pocket to keep from reaching for her.

"So, I really didn't have big plans for this evening, but I need to get you out of here for a while. Let me take you for a drive."

Relief eased the lines of tension on her face. "You don't have to. I do appreciate you going along with it at the table, though."

"If you don't want to go anywhere with me, say so."

Her mouth stayed closed.

"Okay. Let's go." He grabbed her hand and tucked it into his arm, giving her his stability.

He drove to the small memorial park where Cassidy and she had seen him jogging. It was mostly deserted but still a public place. Neither of them spoke until he parked. "You want to stretch your legs a little?"

She nodded, and they got out. He took her hand again, skin sliding against skin, an intimate connection. He allowed their joined fingers to swing between their bodies as they walked along the path.

"You were telling me about Janice," Dusty said so softly he almost missed it.

He glanced down at her, thinking she would have forgotten. Stopping on the footbridge over the creek, he turned to face her, leaning against the railing. The gurgle of the water filled the evening with happy music, and it struck him then how romantic the setting was—fading sky, beautiful woman, water sounds. The slight scent of cut grass on the breeze mixing with the other earthy scents of summer. It was a little early in the season for lightning bugs, but he saw an occasional glow.

He leaned his head back, not sure he wanted to go into Janice. It could ruin the evening. How long had it been since he thought of her and had pain slice through him? She'd come to his mind quite a bit since he'd met Dusty, and it was like he prepared for the pain, expected it, then just assumed it was there. But it wasn't. Not as bad. Maybe some of it would never leave. Her screams. The stench. The burning pain in his legs.

"We were both medical students. Second year."

Dusty nodded. "You said something about that in therapy. You really were going to be a doctor?"

"Yes." Back in some other lifetime. "We were engaged, but we weren't expecting to actually get married until we were settled in our residencies or maybe even later. We hadn't set a date."

Their hands, still linked together, rested on the handrail. Dusty stared at their fingers before lifting her eyes. "Go on?"

He shrugged, not wanting to get into the details of that day. Janice's airplane. The beautiful, dark blue sky. How free it felt to be flying with the woman he loved. How he'd trusted and admired her skill at the controls. How proud he'd been of the multitalented woman who had chosen him.

All of that shattered as the engine sputtered, died, restarted, died again. The fear. The panic. Janice's calm control. Her hands shook, but her assurance that they would survive never wavered. They didn't say goodbye. They didn't think they were going to die.

He breathed out. "We were in an accident, and she didn't make it."

Dusty's head tilted like she knew it wasn't everything. She waited.

"She survived the accident. I was able to pull her from the wreckage. But she died shortly after." He met her eyes as he spoke, hoping she understood why, even if he wasn't her therapist, being with her would be almost impossible for him. What she did was dangerous, and she could die any time. She almost did.

Dusty's hand squeezed his. "I'm sorry."

"Yeah. It was hard. But it was a lot of years ago, and honestly, time really does heal, if you let it."

They stood in silence for a while, the creek gurgling beneath them, their hands joined. Dusty's thumb rubbed back and forth, slow and light, over his skin. The change from comforting to attraction snuck up on him.

His breath quickened, and he swallowed.

He straightened. "Let's get an ice cream before I take you home."

~

THE TRAFFIC WASN'T bad for a Saturday morning, and Roland pulled into Dusty's drive shortly after ten. He hadn't even made it out of his car when she came down the walk around the side of the house. No brace.

Roland stared at her as he closed his door and walked slowly forward. She'd done everything perfectly so far. Why jeopardize her recovery now?

He understood. Or at least thought he did. She didn't want to look weak to her fellow competitors. That's what he figured. He could be wrong.

He stopped with his arms crossed. He wasn't her dad, and he didn't want to be. Should he let his therapist side come out? Or the friend side? While his mind debated, his heart admired her in her blue jeans and t-shirt. Slender and graceful, with an inner strength he greatly admired. Her blond hair was caught up in the normal ponytail. If she let it down, it would probably hang past her waist in a graceful waterfall. He'd love to see it.

Looking at Dusty, he had totally forgotten his inner turmoil. In the end, the words just came. "Where are your braces?"

"In the house," she said flippantly, like she didn't know why he'd asked.

He put his hands on her shoulders, waiting until she met his eyes. "Don't do this."

"What?" she asked, her blue eyes huge. He wasn't falling for the innocent act.

"It's a really bad idea to ditch your braces when you're going out with your therapist."

"Oh." Her brows raised in surprise. He found himself getting lost in her eyes. "This is a date?"

"It could be…if you wear your braces." The words came out soft and low. He didn't even know he could speak in a tone like that. He certainly hadn't meant to bargain with her about wearing her braces. Like she would even care if he offered to make it a date.

But she bit her lip. He could feel her wavering—she really didn't want to do irreparable damage to her body because of her pride—so he pushed. She was always alone, no family to support her, no one standing by her. Maybe the promise of someone having her back would overshadow the weakness she felt over a body that wasn't healed.

He tried softening his hands and running them over her shoulders and around her neck. Feeling soft skin with his fingertips. "No one today will know I'm your therapist. So, let's just have a good time. We'll call it a date, and we'll forget about all the complications and enjoy ourselves. Together. With your braces on."

"I could pretend to be your boyfriend, too."

Shock coursed through Roland's body at Tucker's voice, but he didn't take his eyes off Dusty. At least this way, Tucker would know that he wasn't overstepping the bounds of a therapist.

"I don't need two." Dusty cut her eyes to Tucker, who had come up beside them. "But you know we're just pretending." Dusty watched until Tucker nodded. "Plus, our eyes are exactly the same. People might guess we're related."

Tucker nodded.

Dusty's gaze returned to Roland. "The kid thinks I'm desperate."

Tucker snorted. Roland grimaced. "That's saying something about me?"

"No. That's saying I need to hire a pretend boyfriend by wearing leg and back braces."

"Dusty, you're beautiful and kind. No one thinks you're desperate." His thumb ran over the side of her neck, lightly. She shivered, and he smiled. Slow.

"Come on, you can help me get these awkward, annoying things on." She glanced at Tucker, who had his hands in his pockets and wore a slight grin. His face was open and friendly. Roland really wouldn't mind getting to know him. Seemed like once he got out of his dad's shadow, the kid wasn't half bad. And he kept saying kid, but he thought Tucker was only a couple years younger than Dusty. Maybe his dad's overbearing presence made him seem younger.

"We'll be back in a few," Dusty said to Tucker.

"That's fine. I'm going to drive separately anyway."

"You don't have to," Roland said.

"I'd better. Dad goes to these wine tastings, and they're not supposed to get drunk, but they always do." He shrugged. "Dad'll call around six, needing a designated driver."

"Okay, then. I doubt the race will be over by then."

"Nope." Dusty looked at her nephew. "We can get a driver for him if you want to stay."

"Nah. I know he's annoying, but he's my dad. I have a friend who lost his dad when he was a kid. He'd love to have my problems."

Roland looked at Tucker with new eyes. "Good point." He put an arm around Dusty's shoulder and carefully turned her. "Don't twist your knee and rip those tendons apart again."

"I have a dad," she said as she gave him a look.

"He's MIA. I have a lot of roles to fill." They started walking back toward the house.

"Just be my boyfriend. Don't worry about the other ones." She bumped him with her shoulder.

He would have bumped her back, but he didn't want her to lose her balance. He realized with the restrictions off, and him free to not be her therapist, this could be a great day.

Chapter Eleven

Dusty surveyed the parking lot as Roland opened her door. He lowered a hand. She stared at it a minute before grasping it. She could get herself out of the car. She *should* get herself out of the car.

But she allowed him to help. There was something nice about having someone take care of one. Not that she'd ever felt that before, other than her friends, who were great, but they had families of their own now, and Dusty felt more guilt than anything when they took time from their families to help her. She should have her own family.

Tucker walked up. He seemed a little surprised at the warm smile Dusty gave him. "Does this place have food?"

"We just ate breakfast," Dusty said.

Tucker took after their side of the family with his slender build, although he was tall with broad shoulders.

"That was an hour and a half ago."

"Didn't anyone tell you you're not a teenager anymore?"

"I ate like this through college, and I know everyone says I'll regret it someday, but not today. I'm starved. You guys want anything?"

"Not for me right now. Maybe later. If I remember right, this place has a homemade soup stand that's pretty good, along with all the other typical food."

"Got it. You?" Tucker asked Roland.

"I'll eat when the lady eats," Roland said.

Dusty almost rolled her eyes, but Roland's face was serious, and it made her feel treasured somehow that he was adjusting his schedule to hers.

"Good for you." Tucker grinned and strutted off, garnering more than one second look from the ladies milling around the lot.

"I guess he could have stuck with us and hoped that one of us paid his way in. He's not a leech, anyway," Roland said.

"No, I talked with him a little this morning. I actually think he's a nice guy. For a bank loan officer."

"He's a loan officer?" Roland asked in surprise. "He seems so young."

"Yeah, that was my reaction, too. His dad treats him like a little kid." Dusty looked out over the full parking lot and breathed in the hot summer air. The sky was an amazing shade of blue with not a cloud in sight. The mountains sat in the distance like guards, keeping watch. The buzz of the bike motors as they made their practice rounds mingled with the sound of the announcer and the crowd of happy people spending a relaxing day out with their friends and family members.

The whole atmosphere brought back every memory from her early childhood of the happy times they'd spent at the track. It was really the only time her dad made time for her. He made sure she never missed a race or practice, and no expense was too big.

"Miss it?" Roland questioned beside her as they made their way between the long rows of cars toward the gate.

"Oh, yeah." She smiled, a little sad. "I don't think I've ever been at a race just to watch. You have no idea how much I wish I had my bike here." The urge to be out on the track, racing with the other competitors, was almost overwhelming.

"No bad memories?" Roland asked suspiciously.

She thought for a second. "You mean from the accident?"

"Yeah."

"Nope. It happened right after the start. So, maybe my first race...I don't even think then it will be a problem. I've started so many times, and nothing happened. I just don't think I'll let one bad start overshadow all the great ones I had."

"That's a great attitude. I've seen so many people who think the exact opposite."

"I'm a natural optimist."

"About racing."

"Definitely. I always think I'm going to win." She gave him a cheeky grin. "I usually do."

He smiled along with her, and she realized that some of the reason the day seemed so bright and her spirit so happy was because she was with someone she cared about. Not that she didn't care about her mechanics, Adam and Derrick, and the guys she knew, riders and workers alike, but Roland was different. Better.

She loved his straightforward honesty and how it was important to him to keep the line between them drawn.

"Hey, Dusty!" A tall, skinny fellow shouted across the parking lot, waving to a group of people walking toward the ticket booth. "Hey, guys. It's Dusty."

Dusty braced herself. She didn't realize she squeezed Roland's hand until he squeezed back. She glanced up, and he was looking down at her in concern.

"I'm fine," she said reassuringly. Either for him or herself. The competitor in her didn't want to show weakness. She already had to overcome the fact that the guys wanted to treat her differently because she was a girl. Now she'd been injured. It could change things, although this group was just family and friends of some of the other competitors.

But all her worry seemed in vain. A few in the group asked how she was doing, and a couple of them wanted her to sign things like a hat or a t-shirt, which was normal, although Roland gave her a strange look when she took a sharpie and scribbled her name while the guy was wearing it.

"Thanks!" The kid was probably still in high school, and he wore a smile a mile wide. She handed the sharpie back to his girlfriend.

"Anytime."

"How soon are you going to be racing again?" someone asked for what seemed like the thousandth time, although she was sure she'd be asked that question a lot more before the day was over.

"I don't know. Soon, I hope."

Beside her, Roland stiffened. She gave him a curious look. It wasn't like she said "next week" or anything. She would listen to the doctor. If he wanted her to take another month or so off, she would. It would completely ruin her chances of winning the championship, but hey, she wanted to heal properly. And, she realized, she wanted to make Roland happy. It was an odd realization, and she definitely wanted to spend some time examining that thought. Later.

More people recognized her and greeted them while Roland paid for their tickets and they walked through the gate.

He kept ahold of her hand, and she didn't let go either. Several people who knew her well gave them an odd look, and Dusty smiled to herself. She'd never been with a man at the track before.

"Hey, Dusty!" She turned, recognizing Gary Jenson, mechanic for Cody Kurtz, one of the other bikers who had been in the accident with her.

Her stomach cramped, and she tightened her grip on Roland's hand. "Gary. How's it going?"

"It's going great for us." Gary, thin, wiry, and short, had to tilt his head up to look her in the eye. "With you being out, Cody's the points leader. We couldn't be happier with where we are in the standings."

"That's great." Dusty tried to mean it. After the crash, she'd gone to the hospital, and Cody had picked his bike up and gone on to win the race.

"Derrick's been turning wrench for us." Gary drew a fry out of the container he carried and put it in his mouth. He spoke around it. "You already knew that, though."

Actually, she hadn't. Both of the guys who worked as her mechanics had visited her in the hospital, and she'd informed them then that it would be weeks before she was back. She couldn't blame them for wanting to do what they loved. But Derrick went to Cody? It felt like she had hot wire wrapped around her chest.

Beside her, Roland shifted, like he could feel her pain.

"We're going to go find our seats," she said.

Gary's eyes shifted to Roland then down to their joined hands. His eyes twitched, like he hadn't realized they were together before.

"I didn't know you had a boyfriend."

Dusty moved against Roland's side and dropped his hand so she could slip her arm around his waist. He understood exactly what she needed and wrapped his arm around her shoulder, dropping a kiss on the top of her head.

He held his right hand out to Gary. "I'm Roland, and yeah, Dusty's been with me for a while."

Gary took his hand. "Gary." He looked Roland up and down. "Dusty's a handful. It's going to be hard to keep up to her."

"It's not a competition. I like watching her fly."

Gary's brows pulled in, like he couldn't understand what Roland had said. Dusty smiled. She couldn't have written a script for him any better.

Gary scratched his nose then shoved another fry into his mouth. "Yeah. Whatever," he mumbled.

"Maybe we'll run into you later." Roland gave a short wave as he put pressure on Dusty's back and guided her toward the rows of seating.

"Thanks," she said as soon as they were out of earshot.

"It was nice of him to ask how you were."

She laughed. "Surely you know guys don't do that."

He squeezed her shoulder. "I do."

"You're different."

"I don't live and breathe bike racing."

"I've been trying to avoid it since my accident, so it's partly my fault if people don't know how I am. Right after my accident, I tried to watch videos, and people would call and come, and..." Her voice trailed off. She swallowed.

Roland stopped and faced her. His hand cupped her cheek. The noise of the track and the people around them faded away. "I get it. I can see you're an all-or-nothing kind of person. You're either all in, or you can't be in at all."

She stared into his eyes, so clear and green, and realized he was right. She'd always been like that, but she'd never thought about it, never realized it. It was true, though. And that's why she had such a hard time having anything to do with racing since getting hurt. She couldn't be all in, so she'd put it out of her mind.

"Is there a cure for that?" she asked with a small smile.

He snorted. "Maybe you'll moderate as you grow old, but there's nothing wrong with burning hot." His hand slipped down to hold her neck under her ponytail. "I kind of like it."

She put both hands on his waist. "Then I won't try to change."

"No." His voice had dropped, and it sent shivers up her spine. "Don't ever change."

As though he remembered where they were, he took a small step back and grinned, breaking the spell that had fallen between them. "Except this." He lifted her ponytail. "I dream about how you'll look with your hair down."

Her eyes grew wide. She blinked. "You do?"

"You're beautiful now in jeans and a t-shirt, with your hair in a ponytail, and that's probably the way it should stay, because I don't think I could take my eyes off you if your hair were down."

Her heart lifted like a bike going over a jump, and she could barely breathe.

His eyes closed partway. "I shouldn't have said that."

"Is it true?"

"Every word," he breathed.

"You've never even seen me in anything nice."

"I want to see your hair." His hand fisted in her ponytail. "But everything I admire about you is in here." His finger touched her chest just under her collarbone. "Your drive and determination. Your easy smile. The way you never complain. How you've overcome your family and made beautiful friendships."

She put her finger on his lips. It made her uncomfortable for him to go on and on, complimenting her. It wasn't something she was used to.

"Thanks," she said. It definitely gave her confidence, though. Coming here, seeing all the racers and crew and fans she knew, having them see her weaknesses had been every bit as hard as she'd figured it would be. But having Roland by her side had been a bonus and blessing she hadn't been expecting.

"Hey, you two." Tucker came up beside them, holding a monster soda in one hand and a massive bucket of fries dripping in cheese in the other. "Have you found seats yet?"

Roland eyed the fries. "Not yet." He glanced at Dusty. "Would you like a drink or something to eat before we sit?"

Dusty nodded. "This way." She turned, her heart full of all the things she wanted to tell Roland, and led the way to the concessions.

Chapter Twelve

Tucker sat on Dusty's left, and Roland settled down on her right. He enjoyed seeing Dusty and Tucker talking and laughing. Dusty's family had not done right by her, but no family was perfect. He was glad Dusty didn't seem to hold it against them.

She took the occasional fry out of Tucker's bucket and munched.

Roland had his arm around the back of her seat, with his hand resting on her shoulder. She felt warm and alive under his hand, and he loved the fact that he had the right, if only for today, to touch her.

He'd been pretty busy building his career, working hard on developing the reputation of being the best physical therapist he could be, and hadn't thought much about settling down with a wife. Kids.

He looked at Dusty. She probably hadn't thought much about it either. Definitely, she wasn't ready to settle down. Not if she was still working on winning a motocross championship.

He looked at the diamond-hole flooring in the bleachers. She was going to be devastated when the doctor told her she would never race again. Unless she determined to prove him wrong. Either way, it was going to be a hard time for her. He needed to be around to support her. But he had to be careful. He was walking a fine line. One that his supervisors would not appreciate if they found out about it.

He pushed that thought away. They were here, and he wasn't going to think about the work implications. There was a chance he could run into someone who knew what he did for a living, but more than likely, they wouldn't know that Dusty was under his care.

If they did, they would assume he was taking advantage of her.

Was he?

He removed his arm from behind her seat. She was laughing at something Tucker said but turned immediately toward him, questions in her eyes.

He smiled and took her hand. Her face lit up in response. Yeah, he wasn't going to worry about tomorrow or his work implications. Dusty would be offended if anyone suggested he was taking advantage of her. That was good enough for him.

"We're not going to be able to see the whole race from here, are we?" he asked as she munched another of Tucker's fries.

"Nope. In Supercross, the races are held inside of a stadium, and you can see the whole thing. It's a different paced racing environment and slightly different skills, but similar enough that most riders, me included, can do this in the summer and Supercross in the winter."

"Racing year-round?"

"Yep." Her teeth flashed, and there was no mistaking the competitive gleam in her eye. She couldn't wait to get back to racing. It was obvious.

"So you never take time off?" Tucker asked from her other side.

"Doing this for me is like someone else having a year-round vacation. It's fun. And I happen to be good enough to make a decent living at it."

For the first time, Roland wondered what she made. He assumed she lived in her parents' house and used at least some of their money, but she had mentioned graphic design, and now he knew she was making a living racing motocross.

"How much?" Tucker wasn't as reticent.

She named a figure that made Roland blink. Twice.

Tucker whistled. "All from winning?"

She laughed. "No. Not at all. Winning doesn't pay a whole lot most of the time. Where I really make my money is endorsements. I'm a spokesperson for a few products. Not huge like other pro sports but, obviously, enough to live on and invest."

"And you do graphic design on the side?"

"I've actually picked up a lot of that since my accident." She looked out over the track area before looking back at him. "I seem to be good at that, too. Website design for small businesses, especially. But I've also done some logos and a few things with my motocross contacts, including bike decals and several helmets."

Roland sat, a little stunned. What Dusty had just said opened up a whole new side of her that he hadn't seen before, hadn't even considered might exist. People might have thought it was a little irresponsible of her to risk her health and life on a bike race, but the fact that she'd been working on the side to get her graphic design business going, and still was making money from her endorsements, made her seem like a serious businesswoman.

He had to admit, he'd not seen that coming.

"Your graphic design is freelance?" Tucker asked. Even Tucker seemed to have changed from the skinny, young daddy's boy into a serious businessman.

"Yes. I built a website, and I have a few ads, but it's mostly been word of mouth and winning bids of jobs."

"What about you, Roland?" Tucker asked with a straight face.

Roland jumped a little. He hadn't been participating in the conversation but still trying to wrap his head around the fact that Dusty was a lot more than she seemed.

"What do you mean?"

"Have you ever considered going out on your own?"

"As a therapist?"

"Yeah." Tucker's serious blue eyes studied him. "Dusty was just telling me that you're considered one of the best and that people actually drive for a long way to come to your group, asking for you."

That was true. He'd worked with several prominent businesspeople from different states, along with various pro athletes.

"Owning my own business is a dream, but there's a lot of skills that go into running a therapy group that I either don't have or don't have time to learn."

"Hmm." Tucker nodded thoughtfully. At that moment, he looked every bit like a top-tier banker. He should get out from under his dad's shadow more often. He seemed to grow up fast when he did.

Dusty picked the last fry out of Tucker's container.

"Hey! That was my last fry."

Dusty bit it in two. "Want the other half?"

He laughed. "No, really. That's too kind. I'll go get more."

Dusty checked the time. "You've got about ten minutes."

"I'll be quick." Tucker got up and shuffled down the row.

Roland put his arm back around Dusty. She snuggled into him. He pulled her closer. She dropped her head on his shoulder, and he kissed the top of her head, breathing deeply and closing his eyes.

"Roland Bryant. You found another distraction?"

Roland's eyes popped open. Abigail stood several seats down, a carton with burger and fries in one hand, a soda in the other.

Dusty's head moved from his shoulder. His hand tightened on her arm, but he felt her stiffen. What was Abigail doing here?

"I thought you had tickets to a ball game."

"I would have if you'd have said yes. But when you didn't want to, I came here instead. My cousin, Cody, races. I guess he's pretty good."

Dusty froze under his arm.

Abigail's eyes flicked between them, widened, then her accusing gaze seared his. "You're dating a client? That crap about a distraction and honesty and whatever was all that, just crap!"

She lifted her hand like she was going to throw her drink on him.

He clenched his jaw but did not defend himself. To deny was to go back on what he'd told Dusty they would do today. He and Dusty weren't dating, not technically, but he couldn't honestly deny that he had feelings for her.

"What? You're not even going to defend yourself?"

His lips flattened, but he still didn't move. Not to defend. Not to deny. There was no way he could do either.

Abigail's eyes slid to Dusty. She took a small sip from her soda. "I think," she said with narrowed eyes, "I think there are some people in our office who would be very interested to know where you're spending the day."

Dusty interjected, "I'm not a patient at that office, and I haven't been for two weeks."

"I'm not sure that matters." Abigail's eyes went to Dusty's brace. "Are you telling me Roland hasn't been giving you therapy sessions for the last two weeks?"

Dusty's mouth snapped shut.

Abigail's mouth curved up. "That's what I thought." She took another sip of her soda. "Hmm. Interesting." She shifted then started to walk away. "Well, Roland. I'll see you on Monday. Maybe." She laughed.

Roland nuzzled Dusty's head. Dusty kept her eyes glued on Abigail until she disappeared into the crowd. Her head flew around. "Do you think she's going to try to get you fired?"

His mouth touched her temple. He placed a small kiss there. "I don't care."

Her head tilted up. "But you could lose your job!"

He nuzzled her cheek. "So?"

"Roland. What's wrong with you? This is serious."

He touched the corner of her lips with his mouth. He knew it was serious. He could lose his job and, worse, his reputation. Everything he'd been trying to avoid.

But Dusty had stood up for him. She hadn't believed Abigail's insinuations, and she'd defended him. He'd liked it.

His heart beat fast against his ribs. He pulled her closer.

"I'm being serious." His lips brushed the side of her mouth as he spoke.

Her eyes scanned his face. Her furrowed brows lifted, and her eyes widened. Then they lowered. She moved her head a fraction, and their breaths mingled. Her hand came up to his shoulder, sliding over it, leaving a trail of heat behind.

"This is an interesting time for you to decide you want to make out," she whispered with a smile.

"I don't want to make out. It's way more serious than that."

"Oh?" Her lips grazed the skin of his cheek.

His eyes lowered. "I can't really kiss you here, though." He took a breath, rubbing his cheek along hers, before kissing her temple again. "I guess you'll have to owe me." He grinned.

"Or you owe me!" she retorted.

"We can fight about it. I'm up for that."

"Where did Roland go, and who is this guy who replaced him?" she asked, her hand trailing over his shoulder and down his chest.

He put his hand on top of hers, stopping it over his heart.

"Maybe I'm just now figuring out how amazing you are." He laughed, and they separated. "Maybe I just realized how amazing I'm not. If Abigail goes in and tells Mary who I was with and what I was doing, then I might be unemployed. Not exactly a great catch."

"Maybe I'm just looking for a good time and don't really care about catching anything." Dusty tossed her head.

Roland's heart dropped. He suspected it, but that wasn't what he wanted to hear.

"I'm back." Tucker stepped into the row. "I bought you your own fries, since your pretend date doesn't seem to have any manners." He handed a boat of fries dripping in cheese to Dusty.

"She told me she didn't want any." Roland leaned the rest of the way back in his seat and tried hard to keep the light conversation they'd been doing so well with. He didn't want Dusty knowing that his heart was angling for more from her than just a "good time" for now.

He wasn't even going to think about the job situation.

"Hey, I'll be right back." Dusty stood up. "That's Richard's sister. He was the other racer in the accident with me, and I don't have his number, and he hasn't posted on social media. I want to go talk to her for a minute." By the time she was done talking, she'd gotten out of her seat and headed down the stairs.

"She took the fries with her. Sorry, man." Tucker grinned. "Maybe she just wanted them for herself."

Roland laughed. He was liking Tucker more and more. They chatted until Dusty came back up the steps. He elbowed Tucker. "Her fries are gone."

Tucker laughed and moved over so Dusty could sit between them.

"What'd you find out?" Roland asked.

"He quit racing. I knew he'd broken a leg. But one of his ribs punctured a lung, and he's still struggling to even breathe." She sighed. "His sister's here because her boyfriend is racing, but

Richard's accident shook their whole family up. Her parents refuse to come."

"I can see why." Roland hadn't flown since the day he pulled Janice from the wreckage. Not because he thought airplanes should be banned or anything, but because he didn't want to deal with them himself. If he couldn't drive, he wouldn't go. He totally understood where Richard's family was coming from.

"She's trying to talk her boyfriend into not racing anymore."

"But he won't?"

Dusty's eyes were on the track where the bikes were lining up to start. "No. She said she'd threatened to break up with him if he wouldn't quit." Dusty sighed deep and long. "I didn't know how to tell her that..." Her voice trailed off.

"It wasn't her decision to make?"

"Yeah, I guess." The two turned to a one.

Dusty's fingers tightened on her empty fry container. Roland reached over and took her hand. She laced her fingers with his, her eyes never leaving the racers.

They watched in silence as the gate dropped and the bikes sped forward in a blast of noise and dust. Each biker vied for position. The race was a lot more physical than he'd expected. One guy did clip another, and they both dropped, but they jumped right back up and restarted their bikes.

The leaders hit the first jump, going airborne with a shrill scream and disappearing over the humps of dirt.

"It's hard to get a lot of spectators here because you really can't see the whole race. People lose interest."

"I see. That's probably not a problem in Supercross?"

"No. But you can't get as much air under your jumps, can't build up as much speed, and it's just not as exciting. Still, it's better than football."

Roland grinned but didn't answer. What he'd seen so far hadn't convinced him to give up his Sunday afternoon habit, but he supposed he could be persuaded.

The rest of the race went by in a similar fashion. They staggered the start, so by the time all the racers were moving, there were bikes going across in front of the stands on a fairly regular basis.

As the race went on, Dusty happily answered their questions and gave some commentary about some of the riders. Tucker had been right, and his dad called, so he cut out early.

The late evening light was fading by the time Roland walked beside Dusty back to his car and they drove home.

Chapter Thirteen

 It was late and the house was dark when they pulled up the drive. Roland parked and started to get out.

Dusty put her hand on his arm, feeling his biceps flex under her fingers. "You don't have to get out. It's late, and I'm sure you're tired."

He laughed. "I'm not going to just throw you out the door and drive away. Plus, you owe me."

Her eyes widened. He grinned and got out.

He opened her door, and she took his proffered hand.

"You've got to be sore," he said.

Every bone in her body ached, and it was hard to walk without a very pronounced limp. "I'm glad you didn't let me go without my braces. If I feel this awful after wearing them, it would have been worse with them off, I think."

"I'm sure of it." He took her hand, his fingers sliding into hers.

A cool night breeze blew across the yard, bringing with it the scent of honeysuckle and cut grass. She shivered.

He slid his arm around her. "Cold?"

"No."

"Scared?"

She smiled in the dark. "I would never admit it."

He stood with her in front of the front door. The moon shone down, putting his eyes in shadow but showing the upturn of his lips. "Thank you for being my girlfriend today."

"I had a great time. Anytime you need a girlfriend, I'm in." Her heart beat faster. That was a major hint. She felt exposed.

Both of his hands came up and cupped her cheeks, warm against her cool flesh. He swallowed. "I just realized today how much I need a girlfriend." He paused, shaking his head. "No. That didn't come out right." He breathed out and tried again. "I just realized today how much I wanted you to be my girlfriend. Would you consider it?"

"I told you I'm in."

"I might not have a job."

"I don't care."

"I might have to hide our relationship for a bit."

"I don't care." She moved her cheek against his hand. "Wait. How long is a bit?"

"If I don't get fired, until you're no longer in therapy."

"I could just get another therapist." It seemed like an easy solution. Except... "Would that go against you?"

"It's recorded. Anytime someone switches from one to another. It's not supposed to be a black mark, but it is." He rubbed her cheek with his thumb. "No one's ever dropped me before. Besides..." He bent down, touching his forehead to hers. "I really don't want anyone else doing your therapy." His face showed his struggle.

"You are the best."

He let out a sigh that was more like a groan. "I don't think you're going to find anyone else who cares more about your recovery than me." He studied his hand on her cheek. "I'm struggling with this because I want you to have the best possible care. I know how devastating it can be when your therapist screws up."

"You've done it?" she asked in surprise.

"I've seen it."

"Oh." She didn't want him to drop his hand from her face. She leaned into it. "It could be a year, though."

He nodded. She hated the struggle that she saw going on behind his eyes. "Let me make this easy for you. If you don't do my therapy, I quit."

His lip pulled back. "Don't be ridiculous."

"I'm serious. I only want you. I know you feel like you have to quit because of our relationship, or whatever it is, but I'm not a victim, and you're not taking advantage of me. I'm a rational adult, and I want you as my therapist. You or nobody. That's my final word."

His eyes narrowed. "Let's give it two months. After that, you should be down to once a week, if that, and well on the way to full recovery."

She was pretty sure he had just agreed to be her boyfriend, in secret, for the next two months. But maybe it was just that he'd be her therapist for two months? She wasn't sure, and she was tired. They could straighten it out in the morning. "So, I can kiss you now?" she said, stepping closer.

He met her halfway, his hands moving from her cheeks to around her waist. "You mean I get to kiss you."

"We get to fight about it, remember?"

"I kind of like the anticipation. Maybe that's actually a good idea."

"It could end up being a draw." She slipped her hands up his back, feeling the ridges of muscles.

"It could. And I could go home without a kiss."

"I could go to bed without one, too," she said with a little pout.

"That's sad. For both of us. Can't we compromise?"

"It's kind of unromantic to count to three." Their lips were almost touching, and she was enjoying their banter. She didn't really want to stop.

"We could wake Tucker up and have him count."

"That's even more unromantic."

"Wow. We haven't even been a couple for two minutes, and she's already complaining that I'm not romantic enough."

"He's already fighting with me."

"How about I just give in and let you kiss me."

"No. I'll give in. You kiss me."

"Spend the afternoon with me tomorrow, and you've got yourself a deal."

"That's your pickup line? 'You've got yourself a deal.' Really?"

"Shut up and kiss me."

He lowered his head, and she raised hers, and she never really was sure who kissed who, but it felt like the perfect end to a beautiful day spent with a man she was afraid she was falling for.

She tightened her grip on his waist, pushing closer, needing something solid as her mind whirled and exploded into colors. Her body buzzed, and when he groaned, pulling her tighter against him, heat burst in her stomach and ripped out through her fingers. Her knees shook, and her toes curled inside her shoes.

He lifted his head, just a bit, and they stared at each other.

It was several long moments before he spoke. "If you'd have told me how good you were, I wouldn't have fought you. Kiss me anytime."

She smiled. "I think you get the credit for that one."

"We could share it."

"We'll have to. It wasn't anything that I did. It had to be you."

"Not me." He grunted. "I guess it's two halves got together and made an explosion."

She laughed.

He kissed her forehead and backed away. "I'll see you tomorrow afternoon?"

"Yes."

ROLAND WENT HOME with a smile on his face. He slept with one and woke with one. He was still smiling when he stopped on Dusty's drive the next day.

It faded when she came hobbling out, chewing on her lip.

He jumped out of the car, his heart in his throat. Had she changed her mind? "What's wrong?"

"I just got a text. Riley had her baby a bit ago, and I know I said I'd spend the afternoon with you, but I really need to go see her..."

No one was more shocked than himself by the next words that came out of his mouth. "Can I come?"

Her brows shot up to her hairline. "You want to?"

He shrugged, like it was no big deal. He hated hospitals, and he'd said as much to Dusty. "Why not?"

She blinked. "I don't know. I guess I assumed you wouldn't think it was very fun to head to the hospital and see a newborn. They're usually not very pretty." She tilted her head down. "And you said you hated hospitals."

Maternity wards were not the same as the trauma floor. He could do it. The smell would give him the shivers, but he could handle it. "It's a girl?"

"A boy."

"I'd hope he wasn't pretty."

She snorted. "You don't mind?"

He walked closer and put his arms around her, lowering his head. "Whatever you're doing, I want to do it with you."

He bent down, touching his lips to hers, careful to pull back almost immediately. It wouldn't look very good on his part if he spent the next hour standing in her driveway, kissing her.

She was smiling when he lifted his head. "I'll take more."

He laughed. "Are we going to see a baby, or are we going to stand here and kiss? Because I can tell you which one I'd rather do."

She tilted her head. "I think we'd better go."

"Good choice."

It didn't take long to get to the hospital. As he suspected, the smell brought back all the old feelings, but the years had sanded off the edge, and it only made him slightly uncomfortable. Nothing he couldn't handle. He supposed, if he wanted to, he could go back as a pre-med student. But he loved his chosen career and had no desire to leave it.

The maternity ward was on the second floor. Dusty made a beeline to the gift shop.

He allowed her to lead. "You seem to know your way around."

"I've been here for Cassidy. And Harris. And Kelly. Twice."

He studied her face. She didn't seem upset that all her friends were busy with husbands and babies and she wasn't. Or she did a good job of hiding it. But not every woman longed for a family. Funny how he'd never noticed that he didn't have much of one until Dusty.

"What do you think of this?" she asked, pointing to a pair of glass shoes holding a bunch of blue and yellow flowers. Three blue balloons waved above the shoes.

He shrugged. "Looks good to me. You seem to be the expert."

She picked it up, taking it to the counter to pay. Again her face gave nothing away.

He carried the flowers, the balloons waving past his face, as she led him to the elevator. They were the only ones on, and he put his arm around her, pulling her close.

"Want me to wait in the waiting room?"

She lifted her face, her brows drawn. "I was trying to figure out a way to explain why you're with me."

He couldn't help himself and leaned down, kissing her lips.

She smiled and put her arms around his neck. "Maybe they won't ask."

He kissed her again, a little longer than before. "Maybe I'll become invisible when the elevator door opens."

The bell dinged, and they stepped apart. She adjusted the ribbon on the flowers. "We said we would be a secret. I don't want you to get in trouble."

He didn't want to get in trouble either. Not in any more than he already was. But he didn't want to leave her.

"We're friends, aren't we?"

"Yes."

"Okay, then. That's what we'll say."

"They're not going to believe that's all we are."

"So?"

She nodded. "Okay."

They stepped off the elevator, and Dusty led the way down the hall. She waved at the nurses and called a greeting.

"This is their room," she said to him before she knocked on the open door. "It's Dusty, and I have Roland with me. Can we come in?"

"Dusty! Come on in!" Riley's voice sounded a little hoarse but very happy, and Roland followed Dusty into the room.

Ben Baxter sat sprawled out in the uncomfortable-looking hospital chair, a small, tightly wrapped bundle lying on his chest. Roland didn't know this Baxter brother as well as Tough, Turbo, and Torque, but he had the same deep brown eyes, and his large, calloused hands looked just as odd holding the tiny baby as Roland remembered Tough's and Turbo's looking.

Dusty went straight to Riley, bending over the hospital bed and hugging her. "Congratulations!" she said softly, with a huge smile.

"Thank you." Riley's smile couldn't get any bigger, although there was no missing the lines of fatigue around her eyes. "He was nine pounds!"

Dusty glanced over at the sleeping baby and his dad. "Oh, my. He's so big."

"Well, he was late, so that's probably why." Riley glanced at her husband. "I think Ben will give him up so you can hold him for a minute. He was going to go grab a bite to eat and bring me back a cold water. You can hold him while he's gone if you want."

"I'd love to," Dusty said.

Ben shifted.

Roland set the flowers down on the windowsill.

"You guys know Roland, don't you?"

"Sure. We've seen him at the shop, and he's helped with the kids at Kelly's center while I was volunteering," Riley said.

Dusty nodded.

Ben unfolded from the uncomfortable-looking chair and carefully handed the baby over. He kissed his wife's forehead, and they spoke low before he came around and shook Roland's hand. "Glad to see Dusty has a man. She's a good girl."

"We're friends."

Ben snorted. "Okay." He grinned and, with a last look at his wife and son, walked out.

Roland stood against the wall, watching Dusty as she held the baby and smiled down at him, while Riley gave an overview of their long night and the delivery. Dusty knew all the questions to ask, and she seemed knowledgeable about labor, delivery, and newborns.

Watching her hold the baby did odd things to his heart, but her face was serene, and he could detect no longing or jealousy, just pure happiness for Riley and adoration for their new son.

Finally the baby started to stir and stretch, and Riley looked at the clock hanging on the wall. "I guess it's feeding time."

"I'll give him back to you. I'm sure Roland is ready to go."

Riley looked at him. "Do you want to hold him? The nurses said to wait until he was good and awake before I tried to feed him."

Panic crept up Roland's throat, burning like acid. "He might cry."

"I'll take him if he does," Riley said with a smile.

He would have said no. He was going to say no. But there was something on Dusty's face as she held the baby and waited for him to speak. A softening in her expression.

Roland swallowed. "I'd love to hold him for a minute."

Dusty's brows raised, but she stood. He came closer, his palms sweating.

Like the little wrapped bundle was as delicate as a newly spun cobweb, Roland put his arms out and carefully helped Dusty transfer him from her arms to his.

The baby was lighter than he expected and warm. He stared down into his little monkey-face and felt his heart twist and shift. Someone so tiny and defenseless, trusting him to protect him, made the weight of responsibility fall like a heavy yoke around his shoulders. It should have felt stifling, but instead, it felt strangely right. A longing rose in him, like a lone wolf's cry at the moon, low and aching. He breathed against it, not sure how to ease the deep unrest.

His breath came in uneven bursts as he took one finger and lightly touched the little cheek. "He's amazing," he breathed.

His eyes lifted, and they met Dusty's. She looked at him like he'd turned into a pile of gold right before her eyes and she wasn't sure what to think or do. They stared at each other for a long moment over the bundle in his arms, before the baby stirred and began to make little mewing noises.

"I think he needs his mama," Roland said.

Dusty stepped forward, and Roland handed the baby off just as reverently as he'd gotten him. A tiny little human. Amazing.

They left soon afterward. Roland was still in somewhat of a daze, never having held a baby of any type before. He'd been unprepared for the depth of emotion that had stirred in his soul. As it shifted and settled, his thoughts turned more and more to Dusty and what it might be like to share that with her. Thoughts he was pretty sure would make her run screaming away from him if she had any inkling he was thinking them.

So he pressed down tight on his heart and tried to find the person he was before he walked into that maternity room.

At the elevator, she pressed the button. As they waited, her small hand slipped into his. He turned, surprised.

"Are you okay?" she asked, her brows tilted down.

"Yeah. Uh, yes. Of course. Why?"

His stammered answer only caused her face to pinch tighter.

"Are you having chest pain?"

"Uh, no. Why?"

"You have your hand over your heart."

Roland looked down. Yep. His hand was resting over his heart like he was watching the flag go by at a parade. He shoved the offending appendage into his pocket. "That better?"

"Why are you acting so weird?"

He had to change the subject. "You want to go boating?" Man, he was dumb. Where did that idea come from?

"Sure. I didn't know you had a boat," Dusty said as the elevator doors opened.

"I don't, actually."

Ben stepped off the elevator, carrying a bag and two waters. He stopped mid-stride, his eyes on their joined hands. When he looked back at Roland, there was a smirk on his face.

Roland lifted his chin, and Ben's smirk got bigger. He might have snorted.

"Your son is adorable," Dusty said. She tugged on Roland's hand, and they walked onto the elevator.

"Thanks," Ben said.

They could hear him laughing as the elevator door closed. "What was so funny?" Dusty asked.

Roland held up their joined hands. "Before he left, I told him we were friends. He found it funny then and even funnier now."

Dusty nodded. "I see." Their hands dropped between them. "Are we going boating?"

"We can. I have a buddy who has a boat. He borrows my lawnmower all the time, so I'm sure he'll let me use his boat. We can take it out on the river." Roland felt like he'd semi-recovered. As long as they didn't see any more babies, he should be back to normal soon. He did make a mental note to never visit another newborn in the hospital.

Chapter Fourteen

Dusty studied the rickety boat skeptically. It was a small rowboat, with just enough room for both of them and a picnic supper.

They dragged the boat to the water's edge. "How about you get in first, then I'll push it off?"

The water was deep and slow in this part of the river. "Okay?" She didn't have any better ideas.

"I don't want you straining to get in and hurting your leg."

"I see. I thought you figured if it capsized, you wanted me to be the one to get wet."

"Ha. I actually hadn't thought of that, but I do see the wisdom."

"Funny." She climbed in the boat while he held it.

He straightened. "Or, if it leaks, you'll be the one to get wet first." He gave her a look. "I know how competitive you are."

"That's one area where I'll let you win."

He stood with his hands on his hips. "The first person to get wet, or the first person to fall in the river?"

"Both."

"Wow. So generous." Bending down, he grabbed the edge of the boat. "Hold on. I'm going to shove it then hop in. I guess if I don't make it, you'll have to row back to shore. Don't strain your back or ribs."

"Oh, don't worry. I wouldn't dream of straining my anything. I'll just drift down the river, trying to catch fish to keep from starving to death, and eventually when I get to the Atlantic, a passing ocean liner will pick me up. Watch for me on the news. And remember, it was all for the sake of not straining my back."

"Someone has a very vivid imagination." He started to push. "Or a latent desire to be on TV."

The back end hit the water with a splash. "Just shut up and get in the boat."

His foot slipped and hit the edge of the river with a splash. Dusty had a very real fear grip her heart that he might actually not make it in the boat. But he jumped and landed with a thump. The boat rocked, and she held on to the edges with both hands.

Roland plopped down in the seat across from her. "There. That wasn't hard." He looked around. "I have no idea how we're getting out of the river. How far away do you think that ocean liner was? We could send up a flare."

She raised her brows. "I think we're outfitted a little less well than the *Titanic*. There are no flares."

"I suppose there's no lifeboats, either?" Roland asked with quirked lips as he took hold of the oars.

"This *is* the lifeboat." Dusty rolled her eyes, enjoying their banter. "Please tell me you can swim?"

Roland grinned. "Maybe we should have thought this through a little better." He tilted his head. "Seems like since I met you, my ordered life has tanked."

"Could you phrase that differently, please?"

He laughed. "I say we row upriver, so if I break an oar or something, we can always float down."

"Sounds perfect to me." Dusty let her head fall back and enjoyed the glimpses of the bright blue sky through the dark green oak and maple leaves. The easy slap and dip of the oars through the water was as relaxing as the light breeze that brought the happy smells of summer mixed with the heavier river scents.

Roland rowed in a steady, relaxed manner, his head turned, watching the bank of the river slide by. She gazed at the play of muscles under his shirt, the flexing of his biceps as he strained at the oars.

He turned his face and caught her staring. "What?"

She smiled and shook her head. "You must have rowed before."

"Yeah. Once or twice a long time ago. My brother and I were in Scouts for a year or so."

"Oh?" He never really talked about his family.

"My parents were, are, pretty busy, and my grandparents are divorced, both sides, so it made for a shaky family. But one year, Gram took us to Scouts."

"Your grandparents are still alive?"

"Yeah. Some of them. We all get together at Christmas. My parents rent a big cabin in Tennessee, and we all gather there. They rent the cabin for two weeks, and people come and go."

"Oh." It didn't sound like a close family gathering, but...

"No one in my family really has a traditional marriage with staying together and raising kids, being close." His eyes snagged hers. "I guess, when I thought about it, I wanted to be the one."

"The one?"

"The one that was different. I wish our family had been closer. If I have kids..." His voice trailed off, and Dusty thought of the expression on his face as he held the baby that afternoon. "If I have kids, I want them to have a mom and dad who are together and who are home." The oars continued a steady rhythm. "My parents aren't divorced, but they were never home. My brother and I grew up in different worlds. Maybe Scouts was the only thing we really did together."

Dusty didn't say anything, just ran a finger over the rough edge of the boat. Roland wanted a traditional marriage. Wife, kids, family. She wanted that too, she supposed. But she wanted a championship more. Didn't she?

They continued on in silence. "Hey, aren't those the picnic tables for Riverside Park?" Dusty pointed to the water's edge.

"I think you're right. Want to stop and eat?"

"You have to be getting tired."

"I keep telling myself it will be very relaxing when we're floating downstream." He angled the boat toward the dock.

"If we do this again, I'm going to take a turn rowing."

"We should have launched from here. That dock will make everything easier."

She twisted carefully to look behind her at the approaching dock. "I noticed you just ignored me."

"I'm sorry. I'm just not sure I can ride in a boat, relaxing, while you row. It'd feel weird."

"Because I'm a woman?"

He shrugged.

She let it go. She supposed she couldn't get upset about it. It was nice when he opened her door and treated her like a lady. That protection came as a package deal, more than likely.

The boat bumped the dock, and he rose, rope in hand, wrapping it around the piling. It was a little more difficult for her to get out, but she managed with his support.

He tied the boat and grabbed their lunch. It was a beautiful day, and about half of the picnic tables were in use. They were still able to get one close to the dock.

Several children ran around with a dog. A couple strolled along the river's edge. Three college-aged guys threw frisbees.

"I appreciate you doing this with me today," Dusty said as they sat.

He must have noticed something in her tone, because he looked up. "Still thinking about the race yesterday?"

"Yeah." She fiddled with her sandwich wrapper.

"You really miss it?"

"In some ways, it's getting easier the longer I'm away. In other ways, the longer I'm gone, the better I get, the more I can't wait to get back." She looked around at the bright blue sky and perfect summer day. "A day like today, it really makes me wish I were racing. I want to be out on the track, practicing. I appreciate the distraction."

His lips flattened, then he smiled.

What had displeased him? Was he upset that she still wanted to race?

Maybe she shouldn't have been so honest with him. After all, he admitted that he was ready to settle down with a wife and kids and the whole deal. She just wasn't. He sat, looking out over the water, and she watched him. Holding the baby today had shocked and surprised him, but there had been something more in his expression.

Her own heart had flipped and sizzled. There had definitely been a shifting inside of her to see Roland holding a baby. She'd sometimes looked at her friends and wanted the baby and family thing. She was never jealous, exactly, but she did want that.

She wanted a man who loved her as deeply and as fiercely as her friends' husbands. But that didn't mean she was ready to give up everything she'd worked for in motocross. Maybe once she won the championship.

Or maybe after she won the championship and defended her title.

She took a slow bite of her sandwich. That would be years. Roland was ready now. Would he wait for her?

She shoved those thoughts aside as they finished their lunch and packed up the garbage.

"Want to stroll for a few minutes before we head back downstream?" Roland asked once they had everything put away.

"Sure," she answered. Maybe she wasn't what he wanted or what he needed. But they could enjoy today together. Tomorrow had its own problems to face.

He took her hand and walked slowly down toward the river. The other couple had disappeared, along with the kids and the dog. In fact, only one table was still in use, and those people were packing up.

"It'd be nice to have a house along the river. It's so peaceful."

He grunted. "I love the water, but I wouldn't want to be peeking fearfully out my curtains every time it rained."

"Good point. I supposed there's a downside to everything."

He gave her a telling look, but she wasn't sure what he was hoping she'd figure out.

"You could say there's an upside to everything. That's putting a positive spin on it," he finally said.

"Okay. There's an upside to everything. Even floods." She laughed. "Because you get to live beside the river, so you have to take the good with the bad."

"I'll go along with that."

They had made it to the water's edge. It gently lapped at the shore as it flowed by, deep and smooth.

Somehow, she had turned to face him. Had he pulled her? She wasn't sure, but she put a hand on his chest. It was hard under her hand, with a strong heartbeat.

She swallowed and raised her eyes to meet his. His gaze was hooded and almost fierce. Her chest contracted, and she licked her lips. His eyes lowered as his hand came up and pushed through her hair. "Someday you're going to have to let this down for me."

Without taking her eyes from his, she reached up and pulled the band from her hair.

Immediately both of his hands were in it, threading through. "It's soft."

She wanted to say if he liked it, she'd never cut it, but just a few minutes ago, she had wondered if he'd wait for her. She couldn't promise a man she wasn't going to be with that she'd never cut her hair for him. So she bit her tongue and closed her eyes.

His hands were warm and relaxed and somehow sensual as well.

"Dusty," he whispered.

Her breath hitched, and she opened her eyes. His face was only inches from hers.

She slid her hands up his back as his lips touched hers. The same crazy-hot fireworks went off in her body as the last times he'd kissed her.

She wasn't sure how much time had passed when he finally raised his head. Both of them were out of breath, and she was pressed against him, unsure if she could stand on her own.

He rested his forehead against hers, his eyes closed. "I want so much more from you than you want to give."

She wanted to tell him she'd give him whatever he wanted. But something held her back. Instead, stupid words came out of her mouth. "What about Janice?"

But he didn't get offended, didn't lift his head, although he did open his eyes. "I forget about Janice when I'm with you."

She forgot about motocross and championships when she was with him. Especially when he was kissing her. But no one had ever stayed with her, not even her parents. Eventually Roland would get tired. Maybe he wouldn't leave her, but she'd be on her own. She couldn't give up everything she'd worked so hard to reach for a man who might not be there for her.

So, she just held on tight to him and didn't say anything.

Chapter Fifteen

"Your therapy report is excellent. You can take the brace off, wearing it only if you're tired. But try not to overdo it and get too tired." The doctor looked at Dusty over his iPad.

She nodded, trying to contain her excitement. There was more, she could tell.

"And you can drive."

This time, she didn't bother to hide her full-on smile.

The doctor smiled back. "I know you've been waiting for that one."

"You have no idea," Dusty said. The paper on the exam table crinkled under her as she wiggled, unable to keep still.

The doctor lifted his brows and looked back at the tablet. "If you want, you can ride a motorcycle now, but I wouldn't if I were you. They're dangerous. However, as we discussed at your first appointment, no more racing."

Dusty quit breathing. All the excitement that had been bundled in her chest drained like a flat tire.

"Huh?"

The doctor clicked and swiped on the tablet, not even looking up. "As we talked about before, you're never racing again."

Dusty's body felt like a cement block, but somehow she got her tongue to work. "We talked about that?"

"Yes." The doctor looked over his glasses. "In the hospital, before your first surgery."

"I don't remember."

He must have seen her truly poleaxed look. His brows drew together. Pulling the tablet closer, he clicked back through. "Here are the notes: Patient has been warned of the risks associated with continued racing. The surgery can prevent paralysis, but the risks of not walking again with another accident, even one with less trauma, is extremely high. The entire team of doctors agree: racing again would result in almost certain reinjury, paralysis, and possibly death."

He looked up. "This is your file. We did talk about this."

At her continued shocked silence, he said, "It's possible the painkillers you were on at the time have kept you from remembering. But there is no note here that you weren't lucid. There definitely would have been a note if anyone felt you weren't listening or didn't understand."

Dusty drooped on the table. How could she have "forgotten" that the doctors told her she couldn't race again? Had she blocked it out? Or was it really the painkillers? Obviously, it was a conversation they'd had since he just read that off her record.

Her racing career was over. She couldn't pass the physical and be cleared to race. She really wasn't going to race again. Ever.

Her brain seemed to be stuck on permanent slow. But a thought nagged around in the back until she finally scratched it out: Roland had seen the doctors' notes. Roland knew.

Whatever the doctor said for the rest of the appointment, she didn't hear. She stumbled out to the waiting room, not even thinking to schedule her next appointment. Whenever it was supposed to be. She hadn't been listening.

Eve, the dark-haired Baxter twin, waited in a plastic chair, reading something on her phone. She glanced up when Dusty came out, doing a double take then popping out of her chair.

"What?" she asked softly when she made it over to Dusty. "What is it?"

Dusty shook her head. She could barely lift her gaze to look into Eve's sweet brown eyes, clouded with concern.

"Let's go," Dusty whispered.

"Excuse me, miss? Are you going to make an appointment?" the receptionist called out the window.

"She's talking to you," Eve said low.

"Not now," Dusty was able to push out around the intense pressure in her chest that seemed to be shoving her heart up toward her ears.

Eve shook her head at the woman and took Dusty's arm, guiding her slowly out the door into the bright June sun.

Eve worked on diesel motors like her brothers, and she was strong and tough. Dusty appreciated her strength as she leaned into it. Her own strength seemed to be gone.

She would never race again? Part of her wanted to know what the odds were. Couldn't she make that decision for herself? Weigh whether being paralyzed was worth the risk of winning a championship?

The sensible part, currently a very small part, told her that was ridiculous, and she knew it to be true.

And her heart...she couldn't even think about what her heart was saying. Roland had known. He'd allowed her to go on about getting better, racing again, winning the championship, and all along, he'd known.

Eve guided her to the passenger side of her pickup and opened the door. "Can you tell me what happened?"

Dusty swallowed. "The doctor said I would never race again." Dusty raised her tortured eyes to Eve's. "Forget my therapy appointment."

Eve had barely shut the door before she had her phone out. Dusty supposed she was cancelling her therapy appointment or possibly letting Roland know. Dusty wished she'd just let it alone. Eve took a few minutes before she came around the other side of the truck and got in.

When they pulled into Dusty's drive, Kelly's and Harris's cars were already there, and Cassidy pulled in behind them.

"Eden's coming in a few minutes. She's bringing the ice cream and chocolate." Eve put the truck in park. "Give me a minute, I'll help you out."

"I'm fine." Everything else the doctor had said was good news.

Kelly and Harris both threw their arms around her when she stepped out of the truck.

"Aren't you two supposed to be at work?" Dusty said, fighting back the tears that threatened to fill her eyes.

"I took off. There's a volunteer at the library. She'll have to handle it," Harris said, still squeezing Dusty.

"We knew your parents wouldn't be around." Kelly's tone implied just a little censor. "And we knew how much this meant to you."

Dusty closed her eyes and let them hold her. "Thanks."

Eve and Cassidy walked around the truck.

"I had already taken the day off because of my kids' doctors' appointments," Cassidy said.

Dusty opened her eyes. "Where are your kids?"

"The Kicking Quilters have them," Cassidy said, referring to the older ladies who used Torque's garage as their sewing headquarters.

"As soon as Eden shows up with the ice cream, we'll be set." Eve joined the group hug.

Dusty pulled her lips back, trying to smile. "Thanks for calling everyone."

"You've been here for us. I knew they would all want to be here for you."

Dusty allowed their arms to seep comfort into her soul. Finally she realized they were all still in the driveway. "Let's go inside."

Chapter Sixteen

Roland set the chart for his last patient on the counter. Dusty's chart still lay where they'd set it, waiting for her to show. She never had.

He'd been able to get through the last three patients after her, but he was itching to call or text or, even better, just drive to her place. What had happened that she'd missed her appointment? Surely, she wouldn't have forgotten?

He suspected it had something to do with her doctor's appointment today. His heart pinched every time he thought of the doctor possibly telling her what her chart had said for weeks. His whole being ached to be with her.

Normally he checked the charts for the next day, just to get his mind focused on the best ways to help the patients coming in, but he left as soon as he set the chart down for the last patient.

Abigail smirked at him as he left. He gave her his most professional smile. Their supervisor was out at a training seminar and wouldn't be back until later in the week. He didn't have to worry about what Abigail might have told him until then. But he was fairly confident that everything would be okay. He was a very valuable employee. His reputation brought many big-name clients into the practice. He was good at what he did, and he'd never stepped one foot even close to any boundaries. He was never late. He was the most requested therapist. He was handed the hardest jobs. It's possible that their supervisor might reprimand him, but he highly doubted it. He definitely wasn't worried about his job. All of his concern for today was on Dusty.

He drove directly to her house from work.

It looked like she was having a party. He recognized Kelly's car, and he thought he recognized Cassidy's.

Maybe a girls' night. Maybe he should have called. But he rejected that thought as soon as it came. He had as much right to be with Dusty as anyone else, and she missed her appointment. So he strode to her door and knocked boldly.

One of the twins answered. He thought it was Eden. She smiled when she saw him, but her eyes were wet. "There's a lot of emotion going on in here. You sure you want to come in?"

"What happened?"

"Dusty can't race again." Eden gave him a level look. "You're not her favorite person right now. She claims you knew and made a fool out of her."

Roland froze. Thoughts raced through his head. He hadn't considered that she would blame him in any way. Should he have told her? He knew it would devastate her, and he hadn't felt like it was his position to give her that news. He had also been concerned that it would cause a major setback in her recovery. He thought the doctors might have withheld the information on purpose for that very reason.

He ran a hand through his hair, hating the thought that Dusty was angry with him but thinking that if he could go back, he'd do the exact same thing. He could apologize, but he couldn't claim to think he had been wrong.

He met Eden's accusing stare. "She's right. It was written right in her record. I did know. But that wasn't my information to tell. I assumed there was a reason the doctors didn't tell her."

Eden shifted. "She said the doctor today claimed he did tell her. He read right from her record that they'd talked about it. She just didn't remember. She's not sure if it was the painkillers she was on or if the news was so awful she blocked it out."

Eden hadn't made a move to open the door farther, and for the first time, Roland wondered if she was going to let him in.

"Is she refusing to see me?"

Eden's eyes widened, and she straightened, opening the door. "No. Sorry. I'm actually glad someone is here. We've been with her all afternoon, but we're leaving."

As she spoke, Kelly, Tough's wife, came to the door, purse over her shoulder. She was blond and bubbly, and even though her eyes were red from crying, she gave Roland a perky smile. "I'm so glad you're here."

Eden backed away from the door and disappeared inside.

Kelly continued in a lowered voice. "Tough said you're the man for Dusty. His only concern was that Dusty wouldn't realize it until it was too late."

Roland's eyes widened at her whispered confession. Tough thought Roland should be with Dusty? He tried to remember if Tough had ever even really seen them together.

Kelly patted his arm. "She's not very happy with you right now."

That made the nervous clenching of his stomach worse.

"But Tough's never wrong." She started out the door. "You are staying, right?"

"For a while." He'd just been planning on checking on her, seeing why she missed her appointment. Kelly made it sound like he should be moving in.

"Good. She shouldn't be alone right now. I don't think she even bothered to call her parents."

"Okay." Roland took one step in the house and met Eden coming back out with her twin, Eve, beside her.

"You've got the next shift," Eve said with a small smile. "If she doesn't shoot you first."

Roland blinked, hoping she was kidding. With women, sometimes it was hard to tell.

Harris, Turbo's wife, met him as he was closing the door behind the twins. "Take care of her," she said.

"I'll try."

She opened the door and walked out. Roland felt like the baton had been passed to him. He wasn't sure if he deserved that trust.

He walked through the living room to the stairs and started down. Cassidy, Torque's wife, was still sitting with Dusty on the couch. Dusty had her head down, her hair shielding her face, an empty container of ice cream held loosely in her hand.

Cassidy looked up at his approach. She squeezed Dusty. "I'm leaving, but I'm going to call you later, okay?"

If Dusty replied, Roland couldn't hear.

Cassidy bit her lip as she looked between him and Dusty. She got to her feet, taking the ice-cream container with her. Roland should have thought to bring something, but he hadn't realized exactly what had happened.

Cassidy stopped in front of him and whispered, "She's taking it pretty hard. I'm not sure which was worse, though. Not being able to race or knowing that you must have known." Her voice dropped even lower. "I didn't realize how much she cared about you."

Roland looked at the floor. Should he have told her? The question wouldn't even have made sense for anyone else. It wasn't his place. But it did his heart good to hear Cassidy say Dusty cared about him. Maybe there was a small ray of hope.

Cassidy held up the ice-cream container. "I'm throwing this away on my way out. Call me if she needs me."

Roland nodded, feeling strangely deserted as Cassidy walked away. There were a few sounds, then they faded as she went up the stairs. Finally the door opened and closed, and he was alone with Dusty. She hadn't moved.

He walked slowly toward the couch, moving around the end and going to where Dusty sat in the middle with her shoulders hunched and her back bent, her head pointed down toward her knees. The silky blond hair that so fascinated him hung around her head like a soft blanket. His hand itched to run over it, soothing, but he shoved it in his pocket instead.

He swallowed, loud in the stillness of the house. She didn't move or acknowledge him. The Dusty he knew was vibrant and alive and met life head-on. The news that she couldn't race again really had devastated her.

Kneeling in front of her, he carefully put one hand on her knee. She stiffened but didn't move.

"Dusty?"

After a few seconds, her head shifted, her hair parted, and her face came into view. Red and blotchy, her eyes bloodshot and swollen, she looked at him.

His heart beat painfully. His arms itched to hold her, but he wasn't sure she would welcome his comfort, although she'd made no move to remove his hand from her knee. "I'm sorry," he breathed out. Not sorry for not telling her. Maybe sorry for not being able to tell her. But sorry that she couldn't race again. That something she loved with all her heart had been taken from her.

Her head moved back and forth as she shook it slowly. "No."

"Yes. I really am. It kills me to know how much this means to you and how bad it hurts for you to find out that it's not something you can do anymore."

She bit her lip and closed her eyes at his words. There was no hatred in her expression. She didn't even look angry. Just devastated, which hurt his heart more than all the anger in the world.

"It's not your fault," she said so softly he had to strain to hear.

"No. But that doesn't keep me from hurting for you."

Her head came up. "You knew."

It was a statement, and he couldn't deny it. "Yes."

"Why didn't you tell me?"

At least he was prepared to answer this. "I didn't know why the doctor hadn't told you. I was only the therapist. The stuff in your record is to help me treat you better, not for me to share."

Her forehead crinkled, and her eyes filled. "I thought I was more to you than just a patient."

Roland swore. This was why he shouldn't have gotten involved with a patient. "You are." He closed his eyes against the need to pull her close. "You're so much more."

"Then, why?"

"It wasn't my place. I knew it was going to hurt you. I didn't know why the doctor hadn't told you."

"I went on and on about how much I wanted to race again, and you were laughing the whole time!" Her voice was no longer soft.

"I wasn't laughing!" His hand had tightened on her knee, and he made himself loosen it. "I wasn't laughing," he said softer. "It sent pain through me every time you said that. Yeah, I knew what your record said. But I care about you, and I didn't want to be the one to dash your hopes."

"I was devastated, you're right. But I have had some time to process it and get used to the idea, and I know I can live with it. The issue that's lingering is that you knew. You knew." She emphasized those two words. "And you didn't tell me."

The emotion on her face was betrayal. Like he had betrayed her trust. It sent burning pain down his throat and through his chest. "I'm sorry. I couldn't."

"I thought at first you were hiding it for some competitive reason, but I couldn't think of any time you've been anything but considerate and kind to me. My brain knows you couldn't tell me." Her eyes squeezed shut. "But there's something else, my heart maybe, that feels like if you truly cared about me, you would have told me."

"I swear I care about you." He moved closer and slid his hand over her hot, wet cheek, into her hair. "It's killing me to not be able to fix this."

His heart leaped when she leaned her head into his hand. He cupped her head, pulling her closer. "I trusted you," she said raggedly.

"I didn't betray you," he whispered. "I considered telling you, even though it wasn't my place, but I worried it might set your recovery back. I thought that's why the doctor might not have told you."

"I know. I believe you. In my head, I know you want the best for me. My heart just hurts right now."

His did, too. "I want to hold you."

After several beats of his heart, she twitched then slid off the couch and into his arms. He wasn't expecting it and lost his balance. With his arms wrapped around her, they fell backward together, lying on the soft carpet, Dusty tucked in his arms. Her tears hit his chest, scalding. Feeling her cry hurt him worse than anything he could ever remember. But there was a coolness in his body, too. Relief that she didn't hate him, that she hadn't turned from him. And hope that she would understand and forgive.

~

DUSTY CLUNG TO ROLAND. She didn't care that they were on the floor. She didn't even care that he'd seen her looking awful, as she always did when she cried.

Logically she'd known her friends were right. They'd comforted her, and when she'd complained about Roland knowing, they'd assured her that he'd not kept it from her out of selfishness or unkindness.

Her brain had known that they were right. But, like she told Roland, her heart hurt.

It helped that he'd come. He had to have left work and come immediately to her.

His arms around her, his ragged whisper of apology, the pain she saw in his eyes over her hurt—it all helped.

He tucked her head under his chin, and their legs tangled together. His arms pulled her closer, and she snuggled into the shelter they provided.

She didn't know how long they stayed like that, but her tears dried up as the darkness fell. The lack of light gave her a feeling of safety, buffered by Roland's arms, and she spoke.

"I've spent my whole life working toward winning a championship." Her voice felt loud in the silence of the room.

Roland's hand moved over her back. "And I'm sure you could have done it. No one doubts your determination."

"It's hard to let that go."

"Sometimes it's easier if you replace it with something else."

"There's nothing that could take the place of what I've done my whole life."

He was quiet for a few minutes, his hand stroking gently, soothing. "Was it the thrill? The challenge? The competition?"

Dusty closed her eyes. He was trying to help her. Her friends commiserated, but Roland wouldn't let her wallow. He was trying to get her to pick herself up. And he was right. She didn't want to wallow.

She'd spent a few hours grieving. She'd need more time...how much time? She wasn't sure, but she'd need more than just an afternoon to fully recover. But he had a good point. Replace.

Isn't that what a rebound relationship was? People helped themselves recover by replacing one relationship with another. Why couldn't she recover from this by replacing motocross with...?

"I love the competition," she finally said. "I love pushing to win. But I guess it doesn't have to be against other people. I can compete against myself."

"Okay. So, we'll think of something that doesn't necessarily have to be a competition against other people."

She sighed. "I suppose I could work on building a design business. That would provide the competition that I crave, but..."

Roland's hand had found its way to her hair, and he ran it through his fingers. So gentle and careful she couldn't help but close her eyes and enjoy.

"But?" he prompted her.

Where had she been? Oh. "But I do love the danger. The risk. That makes the victory sweeter."

"You probably won't get that in the design business. Unless you get hired by a drug lord. Do they have websites?" Roland asked with a lot of humor in his voice.

She smiled, surprised, because a few hours ago, she would have said that it would be a long time before she smiled again. Yet, here she was.

"I don't think that's the kind of danger I'm looking for."

He breathed out an exaggerated sigh of relief. "I'm happy about that. I'd hate to get kidnapped and held as ransom just because they didn't like the font you'd used."

She chuckled with him.

He cleared his throat. "Quit making jokes. I'm trying to figure out a new, slightly dangerous, competitive activity that will keep my fake girlfriend happy but also safe."

Maybe it was time to lose the "fake" part of girlfriend. But she kept her mouth closed. After all, if they hadn't had more than a patient-therapist relationship to begin with, she wouldn't have felt betrayed when he didn't tell her what was in her chart.

She let it go.

"Mountain climbing?" Roland asked.

"Hey, that's not a bad idea. We could do that together."

"I'd hike up the Appalachians. Nothing bigger."

"If you're mountain climbing, the goal has to be Everest." She shrugged. "Aim for the top."

Roland gave a little snort. "It's kind of hard for me to believe that motocross is out but mountain climbing is in, anyway. What, exactly, did the doctor say?"

"He didn't say no mountain climbing."

"Maybe he didn't feel like he had to go through the whole shebang of what you couldn't do," Roland said reasonably.

Dusty stuck out her chin, even though he couldn't see it. "Then maybe he should know me better, because if he didn't say no, then I assumed it's a yes."

His hand smoothed down her hair, holding the back of her head, like he could protect her. "I'm definitely talking to that doctor."

He could, too. And probably would.

"Whoa. You cannot use your job to manipulate your fake girlfriend."

"When it comes to fake girlfriends, I need to use everything at my disposal. This is rough territory."

"What's that supposed to mean?"

He moved so that his forehead and nose touched hers. "It means, Dusty Gibson, that I care about you, and I don't want anything to happen to you. And if I need to talk to your doctor so that we know exactly what is going to keep you safe, then I will."

"But you're the one who said I should replace motocross with something else."

"Me. You can replace motocross with me," he said, just before he lowered his head even more and ended the argument.

Chapter Seventeen

A long time later, Roland pulled back. Their lips still clung, and Dusty pressed forward, placing small kisses on the corners of his mouth, unwilling to stop.

Kissing on the floor held certain advantages, like taking away the fear of falling when her head swam and her knees felt weak.

Roland returned each small kiss with one of his own. "With you, one kiss always feels like more."

"I never told you to stop," she said, running her hand up over his biceps and shoulder.

"If I don't stop now, I might not be able to later." His statement was punctuated by his rumbling stomach.

"Oh! I bet you never ate dinner."

"No. I guess I am kind of hungry."

"I don't even know what time it is. Must be late." She tried to untangle her legs from his.

"It's almost eleven."

"I can make you a sandwich."

"I can make my own sandwich. You can keep me company."

She laughed as they sat up then managed to stand.

"Hang on," he said, and a few seconds later, his flashlight app lit up.

"There we go. Now you can walk without me worrying you'll run into something and reinjure yourself."

"When is that worry going to go away? I'm going to have a hard time climbing mountains if you won't even let me navigate my living room by myself."

His hand slid under her hair to grip the back of her neck. "It's probably never going to go completely away. Is it so awful that I want to protect you?"

With those words, she remembered Janice and how she'd died in the same accident he survived. He'd never given her details, but it had to be hard to know he couldn't save her.

"I'm not really used to anyone caring," she finally said.

"I don't want to smother you, but you're gonna know I care."

She smiled. His face looked craggy and fierce in the sharp light. "I like that you care."

"Maybe something other than mountain climbing?"

"Maybe," she agreed, picking her way around the coffee table and walking out to the kitchen where she flipped the small over-the-sink light on and opened the fridge.

He came around behind her, his arms enclosing her. She leaned back into him, thankful to have someone behind her who would catch her when she fell. Like today.

"I said, I'd do it," he growled in her ear.

"Your bear voice doesn't scare me," she replied flippantly, leaning forward to grab cold cuts and mayo.

He moved back. "Really? I'll have to work on that."

She laughed, closing the fridge as he walked to the counter and grabbed bread.

"Are you eating too?" he asked.

To her surprise, she was actually hungry. "Yeah. I think I will."

He grinned, looking her over. "You seem a little happier." He set the bread down and opened the bag. "Now, I know your friends were here, but I'm just thinking it was me kissing you that made all the difference."

She laughed outright. "Nope. It was the idea that I could replace motocross with something else. Something challenging. Something I can push myself to win on."

He spun around. "What?" He stalked toward her. "I'm thinking I didn't kiss you long enough or hard enough if you've got any thoughts left in your head. Any."

He put his hands on her shoulders.

She wrapped her arms around his neck. "I was kidding. It was your kiss. It was definitely your kiss that made me smile."

～

Dusty woke up in her bed, the memory of the day before in fragments. The devastation of finding out she would never race again, the anger at Roland for not telling her. Her friends' support. Roland's tender care and sweet teasing.

His replacement suggestion.

His kiss.

She stretched and rolled, pulling the covers more snugly around her. Before he'd gone, he'd let her know that he hadn't gotten into any trouble at work over Abigail, and with his words of encouragement in her ear and her lips still tingling from his kiss, he'd left.

She'd thought of something to replace motocross. She'd actually thought of it the night before, but she didn't want to say anything to Roland. First of all, it'd been years since her last lesson. And secondly, she wanted to surprise him.

He had so much confidence and faith in her. And not only that, but he'd been so supportive, not only with her therapy and with helping her, but he'd spent the entire evening holding her last night. Teasing her out of her funk. Kissing her...

She wanted to make him smile.

And she was going to start today. She'd taken lessons for a year back when she was eighteen. As soon as she got up, she was going to look up the number for the regional airport and see if Whiff was still there giving flying lessons.

～

THURSDAY MORNING, Roland dropped his car off at Tough's shop for tires. He rode to work with Matt who worked in imaging. They weren't late, but normally Roland walked in at least thirty minutes early, not at one minute 'til.

As soon as he walked into the office, the ominous air hit him. There was no chatter. No one greeted him. Even Abigail stood in a corner, her head buried in a chart.

Roland had the strongest urge to turn around and walk back out, closing the door behind him. But he'd not gotten where he was by avoiding the hard thing, so he walked in, his head up. This had to be about him. And it was almost certainly about his relationship with Dusty. Today was the first day his supervisor, Craig, was back. Abigail was in too convenient of a position for her to have not told on him.

He walked to the small kitchen room and put his lunch in the fridge. He didn't even have the door shut when he heard Craig's voice. "Has he gotten here, yet?"

Craig hadn't said a name. Roland didn't need him to. "I'm in here."

The doorway darkened. Roland's chest darkened in the same manner. He turned.

"I need to see you in my office."

Roland lifted his chin and followed him out.

Craig waited for him to walk through. The office had a shelf of books on one wall and a large picture of the ocean on the other. Several plants sat in stands on the floor. A large window looked out over the green grass behind the building.

Craig carefully closed the door behind himself and walked to his desk. Roland didn't sit down, and Craig didn't invite him to. Craig leaned his butt against the corner of the desk and folded his hands over his chest.

"I have a problem." Craig finally spoke.

Roland kept his gaze level. He didn't flinch or look away.

Craig sighed. "A big problem."

Roland waited.

"Here's my dilemma. This week while I was gone, I got two phone calls. One from a professional football team. One of their guys lives not far from here, and he hurt himself this past season. He's been working with the team therapist, but it's getting to be a hassle, and he wants someone closer. They want to transfer him to our practice." Here Craig paused. His stare seemed to intensify. "To you. They specifically asked for you."

Roland allowed one side of his mouth to curve up. It was a huge honor, and they both knew it.

"I got another phone call from the state college here in town. Their nationally ranked girls' basketball team wants to use us as their official therapy center. Again, you. They mentioned you specifically."

Roland waited. Craig wasn't smiling, and this was all big news. There should be smiles. Obviously, there was another shoe that was going to drop.

"But I received a report, via email, yesterday. A person in this office claims they saw you with a client. Kissing her. That's going to be a little hard to explain to the girls' basketball team, especially." He tilted his head. "Actually, I guess I only assumed the client you were kissing was a woman." He waited with brows lifted.

Roland didn't bother to answer his implied question.

"This accusation is not only hard to explain, it's going to devastate your career. Unfortunately, it could also bankrupt our therapy center as well. We depend on these sports teams in the area to look to us. Currently, you're the one that draws them in." He paused, a shadow of fear crossing his face before he schooled his features. "Roland. I need to know. Is the report wrong? Did anyone else see? Can we deny it?"

The murmur of voices came through the door. Something clicked. Craig's desk creaked as he shifted on it.

"Abigail saw me with Dusty Gibson last weekend."

Recognition flared in Craig's eyes.

"Dusty was a client here. She wasn't allowed to drive, and getting a ride here was burdensome for her."

Craig listened intently.

"Full disclosure, though. I offered to do therapy at home with her, under the umbrella of our group." He had never been inappropriate with Dusty during the therapy sessions. "Billed through our group, of course."

Craig's face clouded again.

"As you know, I have my own business license and have done private sessions in the past. Since she already started here as a client, I didn't take her away but billed her insurance company at the home therapy rate."

Craig nodded.

"She took me up on it, and I've been doing therapy with her at her home for the last few weeks." He faced Craig, head-on. "And yes, I was out with her this weekend, and yes, I kissed her." Multiple times.

He didn't bother to mention Abigail's proposition to him—asking him out on a date with her last Friday in the office. It was at the end of the day. Although it might be technically against the rules, it didn't bother him, and he wasn't going to report it. It felt too much like tit for tat back in elementary school. If it bothered him, he should have, and would have, reported it at the time. Not waited until a convenient time to get her in trouble.

Craig rubbed his chin. "I don't suppose you're married to Dusty?"

Roland snorted. "No." The idea was not repulsive. Not to him.

"Because that would make this whole thing go away. If you two were married, there would be no issue. You can kiss your wife anytime."

"We're not."

Craig continued to look at him with lifted brows.

"We have no plans in that direction." Dusty didn't want to be married. She had a new mountain to climb. Hopefully figuratively speaking.

"Could you be persuaded? If I can say you're married, I don't have to say exactly when it happened, and this whole thing could go away."

"I'd marry her today, if I could. She's not ready, and I'm not pushing her. Not to save my butt."

"I don't care about your butt. It's your reputation that's at stake."

"I'm not sacrificing Dusty on the altar of my reputation."

"What about the altar of this therapy group?"

"Dusty is more important."

"Then she's a fool if she won't marry a man who would sacrifice his career for her."

"She's not going to find out about any sacrifices on my part." He lowered his chin, his eyes dark. "She'd better not."

Craig held up his hands. "Fine. Whatever. If you're kissing her off the clock, that's technically fine. However, if this thing blows up, I have no choice but to fire you."

The back room was deserted when Roland walked out of Craig's office. Although he was already behind schedule, Roland walked to the small kitchen area and pulled a water out. He should be more upset about possibly losing his job. It should bother him. He should be scared and devastated, but he almost felt like it was time to move on anyway. Maybe that was the restlessness that he'd felt since being with Dusty.

He didn't hear Abigail come in, but when he turned, she stood in the door. Anger surged hot inside of him. Why had she felt the need to run to Craig about what he was doing when she knew she'd broken the rules, too?

She bit her lip. Her smirk had been replaced by an expression that looked almost contrite. His anger still simmered inside.

"You didn't tell on me," she said softly.

"No."

"Why not?"

He told her the truth. "If it bothered me, I would have reported it when you did it. You accepted my no, and that's all there was."

She nodded. "I see."

He figured she did. He still didn't trust her.

She looked at him from under her lashes. "I know you're angry at me, but I think I can fix this." Her expression shifted, and he caught a glimpse of the sly woman he knew her to be. "I need a favor from you."

The anger in his chest bubbled and popped. How could she think that he'd do a favor for her now?

He waited.

"The blond guy that was with you on Saturday?"

Tucker. She had to be talking about Tucker.

"He drove a Jaguar?" she prompted when he didn't respond.

Had Tucker been driving a Jaguar? He hadn't noticed. He raised one brow.

"Set me up with him, and I'll tell Craig that I'll go on record saying that I originally thought it was you and Dusty, but in hindsight, I was wrong."

He flinched at Dusty's name. It was one thing for him to lose his career. A huge thing, no mistake. But Dusty was so much more important that he couldn't even begin to match the depth of emotion he felt when Abigail said her name. Protective feelings rose up hot and strong within him. He'd do whatever it took to keep her safely out of this.

He would call Tucker and see if he'd go along with this. If he would, it would keep Dusty from ever hearing about any of it. She had enough to deal with.

"I'll see what I can do."

Abigail's smirk was back. Roland made a mental note to warn Tucker about her, to caution him not to let his guard down with her.

"I can't make him fall for you," he added.

"I know. All I ask is a chance. A date. The rest is up to me. If you get me that far, I will do exactly what I just said and make sure Craig knows there is nothing to that email I sent him."

"I want it in writing."

"I'll copy you on the email."

<h1 style="text-align:center">Chapter Eighteen</h1>

Roland thanked Matt for the ride and got out in front of Tough's garage. The big overhead door was open, and he could hear the old men arguing from out here. He came to a stop when he saw a Harley sitting on the far side of the garage door with a For Sale sign stuck to the handlebars. Nothing fancy, but still a Harley.

He'd never been in Dusty's garage, and she'd only this week been given the okay to start driving. If she hadn't been joking about riding it to therapy and she really had a bike, he'd never seen it.

The doctor had told her "no racing" not "no riding motorcycles." Maybe this was something she could do to take the place of motocross.

He walked over and walked around the bike before shaking his head and stepping into the cool interior of the garage.

His car sat in the far bay, the tires on. The old men at the checkerboard didn't even look up, let alone stop arguing. Tough wasn't out in the garage, so Roland walked to his office door. The old men never noticed him. He smiled to himself, wondering if that would be him some day.

Tough's door was cracked, and Roland knocked lightly before pushing it open. Tough sat at his computer, typing away. He looked up

128

and nodded before finishing what he was typing and pushing back from the desk.

"Car's done."

Roland walked in and pulled the door closed behind him. Not latching it, but keeping out the arguing of the old men. "Yeah. I saw." He handed his card over. "I didn't see an invoice, but you always treat me fair. Run it before I leave, and I won't have to send a check."

Tough did some clicking before swiping Roland's card on his portable reader and printing out a receipt. He handed the card back.

"Saw the bike out front."

Tough pushed back, rolling his chair back and pulling the receipt out of the printer. He held it in his hand for a moment before looking at Roland with a considering gaze. "I think she'd like it. Matches the one she has." He handed Roland the receipt.

Roland grunted, taking the paper. Tough always seemed to be two steps ahead of him. "I wasn't sure she had one. Never been in her garage." He looked at the desk where a picture of Kelly holding their kids was framed. "I've never ridden one, don't know anything about them."

Tough's serious brown eyes narrowed. "Might be time to take a few chances."

Roland had the feeling he meant more than buying a bike he didn't know anything about.

Tough went on. "Kid that's selling it is a good guy. Bought it new and can't afford the payments. He's selling it for what he owes. It's a good deal."

That was more talking than Roland usually heard from Tough. He nodded, trying to look like he knew what he was doing.

"She's perfect for you. Maybe a bit fast, but don't let that scare you. Like I said, might be time to take a few chances."

Roland stared at Tough. He'd thought at first he was talking about the bike, but after studying the expression on Tough's face, he wasn't so sure. Actually, he was pretty sure he *wasn't* talking about the bike. Tough hadn't said Dusty's name once. But maybe he shouldn't have to.

Roland thanked him and walked out, considering.

He wasn't exactly a conservative bookkeeper who was afraid of his own shadow. What was Tough trying to say?

〜

DUSTY STRETCHED and turned off her computer. The last few weeks had flown by. She only needed therapy once a week, but she still saw Roland almost every day. He was coming over this evening, in fact. He'd said he had a surprise for her.

Well, she had a surprise for him, too.

She'd been taking flying lessons every morning. Everything she'd learned from her lessons a few years ago came back fairly easily, and her instructor, Whiff, had told her she was ready to man the controls herself. He'd also said she could bring along a guest. Whiff would be with them, but she could still hardly contain her excitement. She'd kept the lessons a secret from Roland, just because she wanted to surprise him—she'd listened to his advice and found something to take the place of motocross. Not that she didn't still miss it. She did. But the awesomeness of soaring several thousand feet above the earth, flying through clouds, and watching the ground race by was more than worth it.

She hadn't decided if she was going to pursue a career as a pilot or if she was going to continue to keep it a hobby. Her design business was doing okay. She could live on the income, especially since she'd gotten several consulting jobs directly related to motocross. Those jobs didn't have anything to do with graphic design, but they paid pretty well. Still, she'd rather fly. Something about being in the air, the thrill, the little bit of danger, and the speed. Definitely more invigorating than sitting behind a computer working with designs.

The only problem with being a pilot...she had a deepening desire to settle down. With Roland. She knew he wanted a family that was together all the time. If she pursued a career as an airline pilot, not only would it take a lot of flying hours, but she'd end up staying in different cities almost every night. With luck, she might be home two nights a week. She loved flying, and to her, the sacrifice might be worth it, but to

Roland? She didn't want to ask him to give up his dream of a tight-knit family.

A knock on her door had her hurrying to answer. "I've got it, Blanche," she called to her housekeeper who was preparing dinner.

It was probably Eve at the door. She had called earlier and was going to swing by, dropping off Dusty's purse which she'd left at Riley's when she'd visited the new baby last evening with Roland.

She opened the door with a big smile, which froze in surprise. Tucker stood on the step.

"Don't look so happy to see me."

She laughed. "I'm sorry. I was expecting someone else. Come on in."

"Roland?" Tucker asked. "Are you and he still fake seeing each other?"

"We're actually 'real' seeing each other now," Dusty said, closing the door behind him. "But he won't get off work for another hour."

"Big surprise." Tucker gave her a grin, and she smiled back. Yeah, it wouldn't be a big shock to him that Roland and she were together.

She'd never noticed the cleft in his chin. It was adorable. His blue eyes sparkled, and she realized with a start that Tucker would be considered handsome by most of the female population.

"I'm actually here because of you and him."

"Huh?"

"Didn't he tell you about some woman named Abigail?" Tucker asked, his brows going up in surprise.

"No?"

Tucker pressed his lips together, but it was too late now.

"What about Abigail?"

"She's the one that saw you guys kissing when I was here a few weeks ago. She turned Roland in, but she said she'd take it all back if he set up a date with me." At that, Tucker laughed. Five minutes ago, Dusty would have laughed even harder, but Tucker, with his broad shoulders and strong jaw, was actually a good-looking guy. She had a bad first impression because of his dad.

"I think she found out our family has money somehow." He shrugged.

Dusty wasn't so sure. But she didn't argue. Why wouldn't Roland have told her about that? It wasn't like they didn't see each other almost every day. Maybe he just forgot. Although she had a hard time thinking that Roland would forget about something that probably jeopardized his whole career.

"So you agreed to a date to save Roland's career?"

"No. Actually I agreed to a date to keep—" The doorbell rang.

"Oh, just a minute." Dusty turned, calling, "I've got it, Blanche," again, walked a few feet back, and opened the door.

Eve, having obviously come from her job at the diesel repair shop, since she had black grease on her face and up both arms, held Dusty's purse out away from her greasy clothes with two fingers. Her teeth gleamed white in her face. "Sorry. I've got the hook, and I'm on the way to pick up a wreck..." Her voice trailed off.

Dusty looked back over her shoulder to see what had caught Eve's eye.

Tucker stood with his mouth open. When he realized they were both looking at him, he threw his hand out and rushed forward, like he was going to introduce himself.

Unfortunately, he tripped over the potted plant on the floor, bumping the coffee table and knocking the lamp off. He leaped to grab the lamp, which he caught. But the tree fell in front of him, and he tripped over it, again. This time, he flew forward, facedown. The lamp flew out of his hand, the cord ripping from the wall. The lamp hit the side of the open door with a crash and shattered into a million pieces that fell to the floor with an elongated tinkling sound.

Silence descended on the house.

Blanche appeared in the kitchen doorway. "Is everyone okay?"

Dusty had thrown an arm up to shield her eyes, and as far as she could tell, she was okay. But a big streak of red was pouring out of Eve's cheek, just below her eye.

"Oh, wow." Dusty looked closer. "Don't move, Eve. There's still a piece of glass in your cheek."

"I can feel it." Eve closed her eye. "I know this is going to sound crazy, but I don't have time. I'm on my way to an accident, and I have to leave. Right now."

"But there's glass in your face."

"It will have to wait."

Dusty grabbed the purse Eve still held.

Eve gave a heroic attempt at a grin. "There will be medics on scene. Don't worry. I'll be fine."

She did not look at Tucker as he scrambled to his feet. She was already out the door and headed back down the sidewalk before he was up and had reached the doorway.

"I'm sorry," he shouted after her. He turned to Dusty. "I should go after her."

"No. She said she was on the way to an accident. Better let her go." Dusty watched as she jogged to the big tow truck and climbed in, moving down the driveway almost immediately. She closed the door.

"I'm sorry." Tucker looked around at all the colorful pieces of broken glass on the floor. "Where's the broom? I'll start cleaning it up."

Chapter Nineteen

Roland pulled into Dusty's drive on the bike that had been sitting at Tough's. He had not only bought it but gotten his motorcycle permit and been driving it back and forth to work, as well as taking it out for an hour or so in the mornings before work.

Dusty didn't know about it, yet, since he always parked it and took his car to her house. He'd wanted to wait until he felt comfortable on it and like he could keep up with her if they went out together. He knew she'd be a better driver than he was, and he was okay with that, but he at least wanted to appear competent.

The bike was loud enough that she heard him, like he'd figured she would, and she was standing on the walk in front of her house as he came to a stop in her drive.

He lifted his helmet up, and her blue eyes just about popped out of her head. He had to smile. He'd wanted to surprise her. Mission accomplished.

"I am shocked."

He grinned, bumping the kickstand down and dismounting. There was definitely a gleam in Dusty's eye as she watched, and he made a mental note to himself to thank Tough. He'd do pretty much anything to have Dusty look at him like that.

She laughed and came running. He grabbed her up in a hug, spinning her around.

"I can't believe you're riding a Harley!" she gasped between laughs. "Is it yours? Did you buy it?"

Her excitement was contagious, and he couldn't stop grinning as he answered. "Yep. It was sitting at Tough's. Tough said I needed some excitement in my life. Or something like that."

"Wow." She strode over and walked around it. "Tough definitely knows what he's talking about. This is about the best thing ever." Her shining eyes lifted to his. "Is this your surprise?"

"Yep," he said proudly. He felt pretty good about himself. This was definitely a great surprise.

Her smile got even bigger. "I'll get mine out, and can we ride together to go to my surprise?"

He nodded, laughing. "Sure. We have to 'go to' your surprise?"

She got a little secret smile on her face and rubbed her hands together. "Yep. And my surprise is every bit as good as yours!"

"You definitely look excited about it." Which made his heart beat faster.

She came around the bike and slipped back into his arms. "I love your bike. I love that you bought it because you know I love riding." Her glowing face looked up into his. "I love you."

His eyes flew open. His arms tightened around her. His heart scudded and skipped like crazy in his chest. He stared down at her big, deep blue eyes. Time seemed to stand still as his smile faded.

He reached up and brushed her hair with his hand. "I love you." He swallowed. "It scares me how much."

Her lips curved up again, and she wrapped her arms around his neck. "This is where you kiss me."

"This is where I confirm that I'm not your fake boyfriend anymore."

"You're my real boyfriend."

He hesitated, but the words on the tip of his tongue wouldn't be stilled. He had to make sure this was a long-term thing. "I want to marry you."

The shock rolled through her body under his hands. She blinked, and his heart trembled. But then her lips curved up again. "Are you asking me to marry you?"

"No. I'm telling you what I want." He begged her with his eyes to understand. "I want to make sure that you know this is not a passing thing for me. I'm not ever going to walk away from you."

A shadow crossed her face, and he felt instant guilt for poking in her vulnerable spot, but he needed her to know how much she and what they had together meant to him.

"You know how hard it is for me to trust that anyone will stay." She closed her eyes. "But I know you mean it. I know you'll never walk away from me."

"*This* is when I kiss you." He lowered his head and kissed her cheeks and the tip of her cute, upturned nose before touching his lips to hers.

She clutched at his neck, and he held her tighter, lifting her up and swinging her around, their mouths and bodies both pressed together while the world spun.

He set her down and stepped back. "If we're going to make it to see your surprise, we'd better go. Although if you want to show me some other time, I'd be more than happy to keep kissing you."

Her mouth formed an "o." "We'd better get going. Let me run in and get my leather jacket and put boots on. Come on. Blanche made a snack in case you were hungry."

He followed her in, chatting and eating while she changed. Then he helped her get her Harley out of the garage.

His life up to that point felt dull and colorless. Riding down the drive, beside Dusty, with her slightly in the lead, gave him an amazing feeling that swelled almost to bursting in his chest. He could hardly stand how wonderful it felt to know that the amazing woman beside him loved him.

He admired her slender form in the black jacket and dark helmet, her hair all tucked up inside. "Keeps it from knotting up," she'd said with a grin when he asked her why she didn't let it out and down.

He needed to buy her a ring. Now that he knew exactly what he wanted and knew she'd take him, he wanted to put a ring on her finger right away. Be a family. Settle down. Be together, grow old together.

Once she showed him her surprise, he'd take her out to eat. They could hash out the details. Maybe he could push her for a fall wedding. A late summer wedding. They could elope this weekend. He grinned and almost missed her hand signal to turn right.

He stayed slightly behind her, allowing her to lead the way, still enmeshed in his daydreams of the happily ever after he was going to have. Maybe they could talk about whether he should step out and start his own business or talk to...

He came out of his daydream with a start when she signaled a left and took the road directly in front of the big Brickley Springs Regional Airport sign.

It had been years since Janice's death on the runway, but he hadn't been to an airport since, and as they drove their bikes along the fence which separated the road from the landing strip, his heart squeezed painfully before it tried to jump up into his throat.

He took a calming breath. There was a restaurant back here too. Or maybe she'd had something delivered to the airport.

Yeah, that must be it. She'd bought something and had it delivered to the airport; now they were picking it up. He forced his gasping lungs to calm down.

The sky that had been bright blue just moments ago darkened, and a chill breeze blew across the tarmac. He glanced at the sky. Thunderclouds billowed in black columns. After the heat of the day, a thunderstorm wasn't unexpected, but the same dark clouds seemed to billow in his chest.

She parked her bike and hopped off, taking her helmet off and shaking her hair out. Her smile had only grown bigger and wider.

He forced his lips to turn up and tried to settle his stomach. She was picking something up. He didn't need to even look at any of the five or so planes on the tarmac, let alone touch them or get in them.

"Are you okay?" Dusty asked, walking over and laying a hand on his shoulder.

He hooked his helmet over his bike. "Kinda looks like rain."

"Yeah. These babies don't like to get wet, but I'll show you how to take care of them later tonight." She waggled her brows at him. "But first, my surprise."

She took his hand and dragged him through the airport doors. Since it was a small, regional airport, there were very few people milling around and even fewer TSA agents. He barely saw the polished floors and high windows. The doors she opened and the hall they walked down. But the choking feeling in his throat got thicker and heavier. He felt like he could smell smoke and the acrid, burning scent of raw fuel. Feel the heat as the flames shot up, and, worst of all, hear Janice's screams as the flames licked at her...

He shook his head. They stood outside now, and Dusty shook him. "Are you okay?" she asked for a second time.

He nodded, his eyes on a man, tall, slightly stooped with steel gray hair, walking toward them.

"That's Whiff," she said to Roland.

She grinned as Whiff strode up and stopped with his hand out. Dusty shook it and then indicated Roland. "Whiff, this is Roland. Roland, this is Whiff, my flight instructor."

Her bright eyes shone into his. This was her surprise and her excitement. This is what she'd wanted to tell him. To show him.

He tried to get his lips to function. But she was speaking again.

"I took lessons after I graduated from high school, but motocross took up all my time, and I quit. After you said to replace motocross with something else, this came immediately to my mind." Her smile hadn't slipped, but her brows drew together just a little, like she was concerned about him. Still, she continued, "Today is the first day that I get to take someone with me." She squeezed his hand. "It means a lot to me, and I wanted you to be with me." She tilted her head. Maybe at his lack of response. "I wanted to share this with you."

"She's ready," Whiff said. "She's got a steady hand on the controls and a cool head in the air." He gave Dusty a look like a proud father might give his child. "I can tell she raced competitively. She's got everything it takes to make an exceptional pilot." He nodded, slapping his gloves against his pant leg. "I've seen men leave the Air Force with less control than she has."

Dusty beamed. Part of Roland beamed with her. Her dad might not be here to share the moment, but Whiff was just as proud of his protégé.

A gust of wind blew, pushing into them and rattling a metal can down against the building. Whiff looked around at the sky. "I'd like to get in the air before those storm clouds come any closer. Or we won't be flying tonight."

Sudden realization made Roland stiffen then shake. He had to get in the plane.

He looked at Dusty. He didn't want to disappoint her or let her down in any way, but... He turned to Whiff. "I need to talk to Dusty for one minute, please."

"Sure. I'm going to go do a preflight." Whiff turned.

Dusty nodded, her face drawn with concern. "If you're not well, I understand. We can postpone it."

Somewhere in his brain, he realized he had been considering making some excuse, trying to put her off, maybe just getting out of it for today. But Roland knew that was wrong. He needed to come clean.

Dusty needed to know the whole story about Janice.

He put his hands on her shoulders, squaring her to face him, then dropped them. He couldn't touch her. "You know Janice died in an accident."

Dusty nodded. Her brows remained knitted, but as he waited, he saw realization steal over her. "An airplane crash?" she whispered.

He nodded.

"When you said 'crash,' I assumed a car crash."

"My fault. I avoid talking about it, and I only said what was necessary to you."

"Okay."

"I'm telling you everything now. She had her pilot's license."

"I thought she was going to be a doctor."

"Yeah. She started taking lessons in high school and got enough hours in to get her license before we even started med school. She loved it."

Dusty nodded. He was sure she could relate.

"I rode with her a lot but never caught the bug to pilot." He hooked a hand around the back of his neck and rubbed, like that would help ease the tightness in his spine. "I don't know what happened. It was right after taking off, the plane went up then came down. It burst into flames, from the fuel, I guess. I don't know. You saw my scars."

She nodded again, biting her lips and fingering her hair.

"The pain from the flames was beyond anything I'd ever felt before, but at least I could get out." He swallowed. "She was wedged between the door and her seat, with the controls in her lap." He took a breath. "Screaming. The fuel must have splashed up on her side somehow. I really don't know. I didn't take the time to examine the wreckage. But her seat was on fire. Her clothes. Flames all around. Smoke. And that awful smell." He paused. "I was able to get her out." He couldn't go into the details even now. He'd been thankful for his pocketknife that day, but he'd never carried one since. He'd never live that nightmare again. "But not in time for her to be saved."

A shudder ran through him. "I quit med school because the recovery was awful and I never wanted to be in a hospital again. My therapists were great, and I decided I'd rather help people that way." He dropped his hand back down to his side. "I'm sorry. I should have told you earlier, but I hate reliving the memories." He silently begged her to understand. "I never thought the topic would come up. But I haven't been in a plane since."

She stepped toward him and wrapped her arms around him. Relief flooded through him. She understood. She would quit flying. She'd find something else to replace motocross. They'd find something else to do together. Maybe mountain climbing wasn't so bad after all.

He glanced over at Whiff. "Maybe you'd better tell him you changed your mind."

Her jaw dropped, and he knew immediately he'd been wrong. She didn't even have to open her mouth, but she did. "Maybe it's time for you to face that fear."

He dropped his arms and backed away. She couldn't mean it. She couldn't be that calloused. Face that fear? Like his fear of flying was a phobia based on an overactive imagination?

"You don't understand. Did you not see my legs? Did you not hear me? I cut off my girlfriend's arm while she was burning to death and screaming in my ear, in a plane that could have exploded at any second. And I still didn't save her." He didn't realize he was yelling until Dusty stepped back.

He shoved a hand through his hair. "I'm sorry."

Dusty stood looking at him, like she was expecting him to change his mind.

"No." He shook his head. "No."

Her blue eyes held his. He couldn't look away, but he also couldn't give her the answer she wanted. "No. Why are you asking me to do the one thing I can't?"

He realized she didn't look surprised at all when he turned on his heel and walked away.

Chapter Twenty

Dusty watched Roland walk away. She should have expected it.

She pushed that thought away. Roland had been scarred by what had happened to him. That didn't mean he was walking away from her.

But it probably meant she'd have to decide between being a pilot and being with Roland.

She snorted. She loved flying. It was as close to racing as she could come, but she loved Roland more. He was already halfway back to the building. She ran after him.

Before she reached him, he stopped, putting a hand to his head. She slowed to a walk. What was he doing?

Slowly, he turned. His eyes widened when he saw her just ten feet away. His eyes held pain and disillusionment, but there was hope there too, and that hope spurred her back into a run. He held his arms out, and she jumped into them. "I told you I loved you, and I meant it. If that means I don't fly, then I don't fly."

He shook his head. There were tears on his face, and she brushed them off, holding his cheeks in her hands. "No. The fear is real. But as I was walking away, the fear of losing you overshadowed everything else." He looked over her head to the airplane that waited for them. "I don't know if I can get on it today." His eyes seized hers. "But I will. I'm not going to allow fear to run my life. Not now. Not ever. I will fly with you. I promise."

Whiff came over. A gust of wind blew them sideways. He waited for it to pass before he spoke. "That storm's too close. I think we better stay on the ground for today."

"That's fine," Dusty said.

"Maybe we could go over and look at the airplane," Roland said.

Dusty's gaze snapped to him.

"Sure." Whiff shrugged.

"Maybe we could sit in it?" Roland said.

Dusty smiled.

"It's not locked." Whiff got a sly grin on his face. "Maybe you're going to want to take lessons."

Roland looked down at Dusty. Her blond hair blew in the wind. She put a hand up to hold it out of her face. He put his hand up to cover hers. "No," he said. "I think I'll be content to fly away with Dusty."

Epilogue

Tucker Burns looked around. This was the simplest wedding he'd ever been to. It was also the most fun. Someone's big front yard had been transformed into a beautiful fairy tale. Tables ringed a carpeted square where a string quartet played classical favorites as well as more upbeat, contemporary songs. Strings of lights hung between poles, giving the place an ethereal feel now that the sun had almost set.

Directly at the foot of the square, his aunt, Dusty, and her new husband, Roland, sat at a table, laughing and talking to each other.

As he watched, they rose, Roland taking her hand, and walked to the grassy area beside the carpeted square. Dusty barely limped. Amazing that it wasn't that long ago that she'd broken her back. But now she was only a couple hundred hours away from being a licensed pilot. Although he'd heard she'd been busy helping her fiancé, now husband, start his own therapy practice.

Tucker had taken Abigail out and made sure that Roland hadn't gotten fired, but Roland hadn't spent much more time at that practice before he'd gone out on his own. With Dusty. She'd designed his logo and his signs. She'd also made his website, which, in Tucker's opinion, was the best website he'd ever visited. In his research for Roland's loan application, Tucker had combed through everything.

In the end, the loan had been easy to approve. On Roland's merits, not because of Dusty.

He'd always admired her, not that he'd seen her that much in person. He'd followed her on the motocross circuit. With occasional visits on holidays. She had fire and sass, but it was tempered by grace and class.

His mother had the class. He looked over at where his parents sat, their backs pointed to each other. But it was calibrated by snobbishness and a short temper.

He lifted the pulled pork sandwich and took a bite, careful not to get any on his suit. After working in the banking industry for the last four years, his suit felt like a second skin. It was great camouflage.

"Tucker, honey. Get me some more punch." Abigail blinked and pouted her lips.

He took her glass and rose dutifully. Abigail was a woman very similar to his mother, and he knew how to handle her. Roland hadn't known it when he'd asked Tucker for the favor of taking her out.

Tucker had been happy to do whatever it took to help Dusty and Roland get together. If there was ever a couple meant to be, it was them. He looked at them again as they swayed together. Perfect for each other.

There were a lot of tough dudes at this wedding. Tucker was in the minority with his suit. A few of them wore dress pants, but most of them wore jeans and a button-down shirt. Maybe cowboy boots in lieu of dress shoes. One man even had a tie paired with his jeans. Another fellow had a handgun strapped to his side.

Tucker didn't feel as out of place as one would expect.

This was the world that *she* came from.

It wasn't hard to find her. He'd been fighting himself to keep his eyes from tracking her movements all afternoon. She wore a dress and low heels. There was no cleavage, and her knees were covered, but in Tucker's eyes, she was the sexiest woman here.

She looked delicate and feminine with small diamonds in her ears and her hair piled on her head, her elegant neck encircled by a gold chain. Camouflage.

He'd seen her with grease on her face, wearing slim blue jeans, and driving a forty-ton truck. He loved the dichotomy. It pulled him. *She* pulled him.

She turned her face as she talked to a blond woman, and the light hit her cheek, exposing the small scar, freshly healed, just below her eye.

Tucker's heart beat hard and fast in his chest, and he took a deep, calming breath. She hadn't looked in his direction all day. No wonder, since the last time he'd seen her, he'd looked like a clumsy teenager and had given her that scar.

Plus, he was with someone.

She wasn't.

There was intelligence burning in her deep blue eyes. Fire, too. And enough rebelliousness that he knew she wouldn't be following any rules that she didn't agree with. There was a woman who was going to forge her own path. Tucker was drawn to her with a force he could hardly fight.

But he did.

Picking up the punch, he set his feet toward Abigail. Unlike Eve, she was perfect for everything that he needed to accomplish in his life. Since he'd turned fifteen and decided the path for his life, there wasn't one time when he'd done what he wanted over what was necessary.

Eve would not be his exception.

Join Jessie's list and be the first to know about new releases and sales on her books!

Read The Small Town Boy's Redemption, the first book in the Small Town Boys series that features characters from the Baxter Boys, including Eve and Eden as they start their own shop in Virginia. Keep reading for a sneak peek now.

Sneak Peek of The Cowboy's Best Friend

"So, Ames, you gonna go shooting with me?" Palmer Olson asked, hooking a thumb in the front pocket of his jeans, his eyes shielded by his cowboy hat.

Ames Hanson flashed a quick grin, her mind whirling. "We racing?" she asked.

"Of course," he replied with the corners of his mouth tilted up and a glance at the four-wheelers he had out and ready.

She needed a head start. His machine was bigger than hers, although her aim was better. It had been eighteen months since she'd seen her best friend. He might fall for the oldest trick in the book.

She gasped. "Holy smokes! Look at that!" She pointed at the sky behind him. "Is that a Bald Eagle?"

She chuckled as he turned, falling for her ruse. There wasn't a cloud in the sky. Not a bird, either.

As soon as he turned, she spun and raced to the four-wheelers. He already had their rifles on the racks, the ammo strapped down beside them. She started it and gunned the motor.

Behind her she could hear him shouting. Something about not being fair, or some such nonsense.

What wasn't fair was that he had more power under his seat than she did. That's what wasn't fair. But it was his ranch, his machines. He'd had the same one since before they graduated from high school eleven years ago. She'd actually had the same one as well. His old machine.

She couldn't complain. Not every girl was blessed with a best friend whose family owned a thousand-acre ranch in North Dakota. Actually, in all her world travels, she'd never met anyone else with that benefit. Palmer was a one-of-a-kind guy and she regretted all the time she'd taken their friendship for granted.

He hadn't caught up to her by the time she hit the bend in the road where it cut behind the corral and angled up between two hundred-acre fields.

The four-wheeler cornered the turn on two wheels. Ames hunkered down, lowering the center of gravity and leaning her body into the turn. The wide, blue North Dakota sky soared above her as she came out of the curve, the road straightening and arrowing off into the flat distance. The ATV bounced back down. She pressed the throttle wide open. After a one-second lag time, the motor screamed, and the four-wheeler jumped ahead. Flat rows of flax and a deep green carpet of wheat flew by as she raced up the middle.

Tempted to turn and look to see if Palmer was catching her, she kept her gaze straight ahead. As fast as she was going, a little tilt of the wheel could make her spin out of control. Part of going this fast was knowing what boundaries she could push.

The wind whipped through her hair, and she couldn't keep the happy smile off of her face. LA was great. Hiking in the Himalayas was fabulous, and winning two Olympic gold medals was awesome, but nothing compared to being home.

She heard Palmer before she saw him. He might have a bigger machine, but he was heavier. Actually, now that she thought about it, it looked like he'd gained weight. Not around the middle, but his shoulders were much broader than she remembered. His biceps bigger. She always thought of him as this skinny guy from high school, but as she'd been living her dreams out in the world, he'd been here on the ranch, running it with his brother and sister, and obviously doing enough physical labor in the process to add a pile of muscle to his lanky frame.

The screaming of his machine grew louder, and he crept into her peripheral vision. The road was straight, the ground flat, but at the speeds they were going now, it would be foolish for her to turn her head to see how close he was. Focusing on keeping the handlebars steady, she pressed the accelerator with her thumb, ignoring the burning in the side of her hand. The competitor in her couldn't give up.

He was beside her now on the dirt road. She didn't have to turn her head to know what his face looked like. He'd be smiling, of course. But there would also be that little furrow between his brows. The one that he always had when they competed. She'd practiced for hundreds of hours to win gold at the Olympics, but there was absolutely no question that Palmer was the main reason she stood on the top podium. His face was the one she saw as the flag had been raised and she'd had her hand over heart as the anthem of her country played. He never gave quarter.

Always having the smaller ATV had caused her to become a better shooter. Flat-out racing had improved her concentration and ability to handle her rifle despite the adrenaline coursing through her body.

What Palmer and she did here on the ranch in the summer wasn't close to an actual biathlon race where she skied, although she and Palmer did race on skis when she was home in the winter. They didn't do the shooting the same either. But it didn't matter. Her competitions with Palmer had given her the grit she needed to win.

Their make-shift shooting range was just ahead. She crouched behind the handlebars trying to wring out every ounce of aerodynamics she could.

She didn't give quarter when he locked the tires and fish-tailed the rear end, stopping right in front of the range. She slid around to a stop right beside him and was only a second behind him grabbing her rifle and ammo off the rack.

They always shot this one in the prone position, wrists not touching the ground. On a good day she could load her single-shot, lever action .22 in 4.3 seconds. Palmer was about two seconds slower.

Drawing herself in, calming her muscles and heart, she steadied her breath. At the Olympics, she was never the fastest skier on the course. This is where she made up her time. She could calm her body, and she never missed a shot, loading her rifle faster and shooting more accurately than anyone else.

She gently squeezed the trigger on the first shot. Fifty meters downrange, in the middle of the green wheat field, her first 4.5 cm target disappeared.

Four more shots downed the other four targets. This wasn't an Olympic race, and as she rose to her feet and raced to her four-wheeler, she gloated at Palmer, "Ha! Eat dust, *Cowboy*."

Hooking her rifle on, she stared her four-wheeler and gunned it toward the next make-shift shooting range.

Again, Palmer caught her just before the range, and again, she outshot him, this time from a standing position. The targets were slightly bigger, but it never mattered to her. She could hit anything she could see. The first time.

The road followed the rectangular field and she took the last corner on two wheels, heading back toward the barn. Half-way between the corner and the barn, she skidded to a stop at the last homemade shooting range. This time she'd beaten Palmer there, and that almost guaranteed her win.

She kept her concentration, though, as she yanked her rifle out and jumped off the four-wheeler. Palmer skidded to a stop beside her. Close. So close she thought he was going to hit her, and she committed the cardinal sin: she looked at him.

Normally, in any professional race, she wouldn't even acknowledge that she had competitors. She raced like she had blinders on.

However, the competitors skied, or a few times she'd competed in the summer equivalent of a biathlon where the competitors jogged. She'd never had to worry about an over-eager competitor hitting her with his ATV.

Palmer didn't hit her, but the damage was done. It wasn't that she looked at him, per se. It was more about *what* he looked like. His plain white t shirt clung lovingly to shoulders as wide as cross members on electric wires. His biceps bulged as he grabbed his rifle. His long, jean clad legs flexed with power and strength as he leapt off the four-wheeler and raced to get in position.

He threw himself on the ground, stretched out, rifle ready. Broad shoulders tapered to a narrow waist, and his boots, worn and scuffed, pointed back toward her. He'd long since lost his cowboy hat and his hair was only slightly longer than the stubble on his face.

In those two seconds she looked at him, it hit her for the first time in her life. Palmer was rugged. Tough. Handsome.

Attractive.

That thought is what made her stumble.

It was a rogue. There was no way she could think like that. Palmer was her best friend.

She flung herself down on the ground beside him, lifting her rifle. It would take him seven shots to hit the five targets. That meant she had nine seconds on him, since she would hit all of hers, and he'd waste those nine seconds reloading twice more than she would have to.

Except...she missed.

Frustration rocked through her. She missed maybe five percent of her shots. Maybe. On a day she had the flu. Today, with the sun shining down and in perfect health, she couldn't believe it.

It only took her a second to set her jaw and adjust her grip on the rifle. She didn't miss again, but Palmer must not have either, because he rose when she did, his targets all shot down, and raced to his machine.

They took off together, side-by-side, and flew wide open the last short distance to the far corral gate, which was always their unofficial finish line.

It wasn't enough for him to pull completely ahead of her. His body was even with her front tire. So, still holding the throttle wide open, she took her other hand off the handlebars and stretched out over her rifle, leaning forward as far as she could. Her fingertips just passed his handlebars as the gate flew closer.

She yelled, "I'm first, Cowboy!" as they flew by it, her fingertips just inching past him.

He turned at the sound of her voice. His eyes widened at her position. She probably looked like a bird on a death dive, but it didn't matter, because her fingers had crossed the line before any of his body parts.

She straightened on her ATV and punched her fist in the air. "Ya Hoo!" she cried.

Whatever little glitch she'd had at the last range was gone, and she turned brilliant eyes to Palmer. His shining blue eyes smiled back at her, even as he shook his head.

They hit the brakes and their machines fishtailed in different directions, coming to a stop facing each other. How many hundreds of times over the years had they done this together? Maybe thousands since she'd decided in high school she wanted to compete in an Olympic biathlon.

Palmer had never wanted to be anything but a rancher on his grandparents' spread, but he'd been more than happy to help her get better.

"I won!" she said triumphantly, just in case he'd missed it.

"You did not. I was across the line well before you."

"Maybe. But my fingers broke the plane first, so that makes me the winner."

"All I had to do was scratch my nose and my elbow would have been ahead of your fingers."

She tossed her hair. "Maybe you should have had an itchy nose, then."

"Fine. I'll let you say you won. This time."

"I win every time."

"No you don't. I beat you once ten years ago, Squeegee."

Oh, he had to break the nickname out. She slapped her handlebars and crossed her arms over her chest. "That was the summer I had a broken leg and I let you talk me into racing anyway."

"I talked you into it, because I had a broken leg too." He lowered his head. "My broken leg was your fault, Squeegee."

Okay, so that was true. She'd thought bungee jumping from the top barn beam was a good idea, and she'd talked him into doing it with her, doubles. "How was I supposed to know the bungee cords would stretch like that?" After they'd been carted off to the hospital, both of them unable to walk, and after the pain meds had kicked in, he'd dubbed her Squeegee. She thought it was his way of combining Squashed and Bungee, but she wasn't sure. Sometimes with Palmer, she was better off not knowing.

Anyway, he didn't use it all the time, but usually brought it out sometimes to remind her of her own stupidity. She wasn't falling for his mind games. "Why did you go along with it? No one made you jump off the top of the roof."

"Seriously? I was a loyal friend, and now, somehow everything is my fault?"

She tried not to react at the way he said "friend." She'd almost lost this race because of the inappropriate thoughts she'd been having about her "friend."

As though he knew she needed a subject change – Palmer could always read her mind – he said, "So, you're really back for the whole summer?"

"Yep." She kicked her legs up and propped her cowgirl boots on the handle bars, leaning back on her elbows and lifting her face to the big North Dakota sky. "There's not a sky in the world that compares to ours."

She heard him shift, but he didn't answer. He never seemed to care that she left for long periods of time since they'd graduated from high school. They texted all the time and facetimed weekly – they joked about their Saturday night "facetime date."

She'd been to the Olympics, to the Himalayas, to all fifty states and seventeen different countries. She'd studied abroad, been runner up in the Miss North Dakota contest, and she'd worked in the corporate world as a marketing exec. All that time, Palmer had been a rock. Stuck on the farm. Content, apparently, with the short North Dakota summers and long, dark, frigid North Dakota winters.

"Working at the C store?" he asked after a few minutes of them lying with their faces to the sky. That was the nice thing about Palmer. They didn't need to talk. And it didn't matter how long she'd been gone, they always picked right back up as best friends and buddies. It was never awkward. She wasn't even as close to any of her girlfriends as she was to him.

"Yeah." Her parents owned the only convenience store in Sweet Water. After coaching the junior world biathlon team all winter, she'd applied for and was now on the short list for a plum broadcasting job at a sports channel located in LA. She'd never lived very long anywhere since she'd left Sweet Water, and she was hoping to get that job and put down roots in the city.

"Staying this time?" he asked casually.

She didn't open her eyes or sit up. They'd talked about it when they were younger but hadn't had the conversation in a while. The one where he believed she would eventually come back and settle down, and she denied even liking North Dakota, yet alone wanting to live here.

"No way," she said. Her lips turned up in a grin and she didn't even open her eyes. She knew what it took to set him off.

Only he didn't take the bait this time.

The silence between them stretched.

For the first time ever, she was uncomfortable with nothing between them, like if she didn't have words to anchor him to her, he'd drift off and she'd lose him. So she opened her mouth, "I told you about that job I applied for in LA. You ready to travel to California?"

The sun warmed her face and neck. She felt the heat through her jeans. But she felt the silence of her friend even more.

"Nah," he finally said. "Thinking I'm gonna get married."

Her eyes popped open. Her heart thudded to a stop and her lungs froze.

She pulled on her Olympic training to keep from jerking up. Instead, she moved slowly, leveling her gaze at him before dropping her boots to the foot rests and sitting up. "We text every day and you didn't mention you had a girlfriend?"

Why wasn't she happy for him? Her brain felt scrambled, and she couldn't dredge up any good feelings at all. Which was weird, because she'd had two girlfriends in the past ten months announce their engagements, and Ames had been over the moon for them. Why wasn't she happier for Palmer?

He hadn't propped his feet up, but he was leaning back on his elbows. His thin white t shirt allowed her to see, quite plainly, that his abs were well-defined. Her heart did that abnormal flip, and a thread of attraction wrapped around it. He lowered his eyes from the sky and looked at her under hooded lashes. "I don't."

Her stomach whipped back like she'd been hit in the mid-section with a bowling ball. "Oh, my gosh. You're gay."

He grinned. Slow and easy, the grin she loved. The one he didn't use on anyone but her. "You think?"

She ran her eyes over his face, down his broad shoulders and deep chest, down to his waist where his jeans sat low on his hips. Her eyes flew back to his.

Why was she suddenly breathless?

"No, I don't. I guess we've never talked about that, though." They never talked about relationships. She'd not really had any. One didn't become an Olympic caliber athlete by hanging out at bars, trying to pick up a date. Not that she'd even want to date a guy who didn't have anything else better to do with his time.

She decided to call his bluff. "So you have a boyfriend?" Her words didn't come out quite as confident and flippant as she wanted them to.

He did the slow grin on her again, and her heart flipped twice. When had Palmer gotten so handsome? And muscular?

"Nope."

"How long's it been since I've been home?" she asked. "Have we started a new tradition in Sweet Water when people just up and get married?"

"It's been eighteen months since you were here," he said. Answering her first question but leaving her second one unanswered.

It had been winter. Palmer would have had a beard, and she probably wouldn't have seen him in anything less than a flannel shirt and lined vest. Insulated jeans and boots.

And before that she'd come back for a few quick visits, so it had been years since they'd spent any large amounts time together. At least five years or more since they'd spent the summer together. And now he goes and ruins it by announcing he was going to get married.

"You're only twenty-eight."

He shrugged.

"How are you getting married when you don't have a girlfriend?"

He shrugged again, the movements of his muscles under his t shirt so fascinating, she almost missed his answer.

"Figured you'd help me, Squeegee."

～

What was a best friend for if not to find a fiancé for him?

Palmer grinned at Ames's shocked expression.

Over the years she'd been gone more than she'd been around. That didn't keep him from thinking about her. But he knew himself. He was as deeply rooted in the North Dakota soil as the prairie grass that grew to the west. His Norwegian ancestors had loved this land, worked it and carved a living from it. He was destined to do the same.

At one time he'd hoped Ames would be too. Thought maybe she'd settle down after the Olympics. But she hadn't. She'd even worked a job in New Jersey for a while. When she quit that, he'd thought she was coming home for good. But she'd just landed for a while, nursed her bruised feathers and took off again.

"Of course I'll help you." She gave her hair a toss. "I have at least four friends who will die when they see you. And I can get my college roommate to ask her sister-"

He held a hand up. "Whoa."

Her eyes danced but she clamped her mouth shut.

"I have some standards, you know."

"Like I would set my best friend up with just anyone."

He raised a brow. He really wasn't sure. Of course, she liked him as a friend, but she'd never cared about his relationships, or lack of them. How could he have a relationship when no other woman measured up to his best friend?

He grunted and straightened. "Come on. I have a couple cows in the corral I need to throw hay down to. I'll tell you about it then." She wasn't going to believe what he had to tell her anyway.

She didn't say anything but started her machine.

That was one of the many nice things about Ames. She was competitive, exceptionally competitive. But she wasn't constantly trying to beat him. They'd race. Hard and fast. But when they weren't racing, she didn't make all of life into a competition. He'd worked with guys like that and they were annoying.

You only got to live once, might as well enjoy it.

They pulled behind the barn, parking in front of the big double doors. Sure, it'd been years since Ames had helped out in the summer, but in high school and even into college, before she went to Germany or wherever, she'd been on the farm a lot of weekends and every summer. As often as she could get out of watching the C store for her parents.

She didn't hesitate but walked with him to the door and waited while he slid it open. "So what are your stipulations?"

"They're not mine."

She laughed. "You're getting married according to someone else's stipulations?"

"Kinda."

"Okay, so now I'm really curious." She set her hands on her slim hips. He figured she'd gained a little weight back from the peak physical condition she'd been in for the last Olympics. Definitely she wasn't as skinny as she'd been when she'd been runner up in the Miss North Dakota contest. She had a few more curves.

He didn't care. It didn't matter to him what she looked like. Although he did love her dimples. One in each cheek and they flashed every time she smiled.

"I got a letter."

"From an old flame?"

"Yeah." Like he had any of those.

Her eyes got big.

"Not really." He grabbed the pitchfork. "From a lawyer."

"That doesn't sound good."

"Kinda what I thought when I saw the return address." He stuck the pitchfork in the hay. "But I opened it anyway."

He'd been coming into the house after a long day of drilling wheat. His sister, Louise, had been there with her daughter, and they'd been talking care of his grandparents. The mail was lying on the counter and he'd grabbed it, flipping through to see if there was anything urgent that needed his attention.

She grabbed the other pitchfork that leaned against the far wall. "What'd it say, and how does this have anything to do with you getting married? Did someone claim to be your wife?"

"No. Nothing like that." He picked up a big forkful of hay and walked over to the open doorway that overlooked the corral, tossing it out.

She tossed hers and grabbed his arm as he went to move by her. It burned and he shifted away on the pretense of setting his pitchfork down.

"Stop. Just tell me."

"If you can't work and talk, just work."

She rolled her eyes. "Man. Your grandmother used to say that all summer long."

"Yeah. While we were in the pea patch picking peas."

She exchanged a commiserating looking with him. "The most boring job in the world."

"For you, maybe. I liked it." Because she was with him.

"You couldn't have. There is no one on this earth who actually likes picking peas."

He shrugged. "I do."

She shook her head. "Just tell me about the letter and what this has to do with you getting married."

The dim interior of the barn didn't allow him to see her face like he wanted to, but there was a tone in her voice that stirred a flutter of hope in his chest.

"You remember Mr. Edwards from Sweet Water Ranch?'

"Of course. The local billionaire. Sold his ranch in the western part of the state to the oil industry and made billions from investments." Ames stared at him. "You know nothing that you've said so far has made any sense?"

"I'm going to make less sense from here on out, so if your delicate sensibilities aren't up to the challenge..." his voice trailed off.

"Oh, I'm *always* up for the challenge."

"Actually, Squeegee, I'm not sure even you are up to this challenge."

"Would you just spit it out?"

He laughed and started back to the hay. "Why would I do that when it's so much fun to frustrate you?"

"Ugh!" She came stomping behind him.

"One of us has patience, and one of us...doesn't."

"I don't poke fun at your weaknesses," she huffed.

"Really? Hmm." He pretended to think before sticking his fork in the hay. "I thought I heard someone who sounded a lot like you saying, 'take that, *Cowboy*.'" He imitated her voice pretty well, if he did say so himself, drawing out the "cowboy."

He picked up his forkful of hay, but she stood in his way, hand on hips. "Spit it."

"Mr. Edwards died. His lawyer sent me the letter. It said he willed me a billion dollars in his will."

Ames blinked. Not the kind of blink where the eyes go shut then open again, but the kind of blink where the eyelids go shut and kind of flutter there like the person blinking was too shocked to blink and process information at the same time. "Did you say 'billion?'"

"With a 'b.'"

"Billion?"

"Yes."

"One billion dollars?"

"No. One billion rupees."

Her eyes narrowed. "Oh, that makes a difference. I don't think they're worth as much with the exchange rate-"

"One billion dollars, Ames. One billion. Dollars." He put the tongs of the fork on the floor, emphasizing his words. "One billion. But," he held his hand up. "There are conditions."

"Of course."

He nodded, leaning against the fork handle. There was silence in the barn.

"Well, what are they?" Ames finally burst out.

He shrugged. "I don't know."

"Oookaaay." She stepped back and he swiped the hay back up on his fork. "How do you find out?"

"I have to drive to Fargo to meet with him."

"When?"

"I don't know. I haven't made an appointment yet." He'd known Ames was coming home. For some reason, when the letter mentioned marriage, with "other requirements" he'd not wanted to move forward without Ames.

"Who all knows?"

"I got the letter last week. You're the first person I've told."

"There's one billion dollars sitting in an account for you somewhere and you haven't done anything about it? You're just sitting here, waiting for...for what?"

His lips turned up slowly.

She snorted and rolled her eyes. "No. Don't even look at me like that."

"Like what?"

"I don't know. Whatever that look is when you curl your lips up like a walrus about to sneeze."

He threw his head back and laughed.

"Seriously Palmer. Go get your money! What are you waiting on?"

"The letter didn't say much, but it did say I had to be married. No point in rushing off to the lawyer's office when I know I don't qualify."

"Well, there's like three eligible women in Sweet Water and one of them is your sister. So, I'll invite a few of my friends up and you can have your pick of them."

"Have my pick? You make it sound like I'm buying a tractor."

"Well, in some ways it's very similar."

"It's not and you know it. I'm not really into the lovey-dovey romantic stuff, but I've been around women," he gave her a wicked smile, "*you*, long enough, that I know it's not going to be as easy as 'picking' her out."

"When they hear the word 'billion' they will line up and let you pick."

He rested his wrist on the top of the handle. "I don't see you lining up."

She tossed her head. "Marriage would ruin our great friendship. Money ruins everything anyway."

He thought of his grandparents and how they wanted to stay on the farm. But it was running his sister, Louise, ragged trying to take care of them and her eight-year-old daughter, as well as work the second shift at the diner. He helped out – taking care of everything at night and in the evenings. But both Louise and he were going to wear out at some point as their care got more involved. That billion dollars would pay off the second mortgage on the farm and pay for a caretaker for his grandparents, too. Without it, his ranching days were numbered. They'd have to sell in order to pay for a nursing home. And his grandparents would hate it.

"Not everything," he said. Ames didn't look like she believed him, but she shrugged anyway.

He shoved his fork into another pile of hay. "This should do it. Come in for a bit. My grandparents would love to see you."

"Your parents are still in Florida?"

"Nope. Arizona now. Talking about trying out New Mexico."

"You hated that."

He had. His dad was in the army and never stayed in one place very long, which his mother had loved, but his older brother, Sawyer, and Louise and he had hated it. Three years in a row they'd gone to two different schools. Each year. They'd never spent more than two years in one place.

It had been a real blessing when his parents had spent the winter in North Dakota. That was his ninth-grade year. When they'd gotten ready to move to Montana, Sawyer, Louise and he had begged to stay with their grandparents. After that, his parents visited once every few years. He couldn't even say if his dad was still in the army.

It had worked out for the best. "We landed here. No better place in the States. And I ought to know."

"I've been around too."

She had. He prompted, "And?"

"That's true. North Dakota is Heaven in a freezer."

Sign up for Jessie's newsletter! Get a free book, access to exclusive bonus content, get fun and funny updates on her life on the farm and more!

A Gift from Jessie

View this code through your smart phone camera to be taken to a page where you can download a FREE ebook when you sign up to get updates from Jessie Gussman! Find out why people say, "Jessie's is the only newsletter I open and read" and "You make my day brighter. Love, love, love reading your newsletters. I don't know where you find time to write books. You are so busy living life. A true blessing." and "I know from now on that I can't be drinking my morning coffee while reading your newsletter – I laughed so hard I sprayed it out all over the table!"

Claim your free book from Jessie!

Escape to more faith-filled romance series by Jessie Gussman!

The Complete Sweet Water, North Dakota Reading Order:

Series One: Sweet Water Ranch Western Cowboy Romance (11 book series)

Series Two: Coming Home to North Dakota (12 book series)

Series Three: Flyboys of Sweet Briar Ranch in North Dakota (13 book series)

Series Four: Sweet View Ranch Western Cowboy Romance (10 book series)

Spinoffs and More! Additional Series You'll Love:

Jessie's First Series: Sweet Haven Farm (4 book series)

Small-Town Romance: The Baxter Boys (5 book series)

Bad-Boy Sweet Romance: Richmond Rebels Sweet Romance (3 book series)

Sweet Water Spinoff: Cowboy Crossing (9 book series)

Small Town Romantic Comedy: Good Grief, Idaho (5 book series)

True Stories from Jessie's Farm: Stories from Jessie Gussman's Newsletter (3 book series)

Reader-Favorite! Sweet Beach Romance: Blueberry Beach (8 book series)

Blueberry Beach Spinoff: Strawberry Sands (10 book series)

From Strawberry Sands to: Raspberry Ridge (12 book series)

Swoonfully Jolly Holiday Stories:

Holiday Romance: Cowboy Mountain Christmas (6 book series)

Cowboy Mountain Christmas Spinoff: A Heartland Cowboy Christmas (9 book series)

New and Much Loved: Mistletoe Meadows (4 books and counting!)

Laughing Through the Snow: Christmas Tree, PA Sweet Romcoms (6 short reads)